The Bird That Swallowed Its Cage

The Bird That Swallowed Its Cage

Selected Works of Curzio Malaparte

Adapted and Translated by
Walter Murch

With an Afterword by
Lawrence Weschler

COUNTERPOINT · BERKELEY

(In the fall) casa come me (through the barbed wire by Tommaso Rositani Suckert, ©Tommaso
Rositani Suckert); Casa Come Me the other photos by Alessia Rositani Suckert © Alessia
Rositani Suckert

Casa Malaparte is a work of architecture created by Curzio Malaparte

"Murderer" (Untitled), adapted from *Mamma Marcia* (Leonardo, Milano, 1990); "Six Winds" (Untitled) from *Maledetti Toscani* (Leonardo, Milano, 1994); "Two Sisters" (*Le due sorelle*) from *Fughe
in prigione* (Valecchi, Firenze, 1954); "Today We Fly" (*Oggi si vola*) from *Fughe in prigione* (Valecchi, Firenze, 1954); "El Traidor" (Untitled) excerpted from *Journal d'un étranger à Paris* (Denoël,
Paris, 1967); "The Visit of the Angel" (*Visita dell'Angelo*) from *Fughe in prigione* (Valecchi, Firenze,
1954); "The Little Hand" (Untitled) excerpted from *Maledetti Toscani* (Leonardo, Milano, 1994);
"Partisans, 1944" (Untitled) adapted from *Mamma Marcia* (Leonardo, Milano, 1990); "Woman by
the Edge of the Sea" (*Donna in riva al mare*) from *Fughe in prigione* (Valecchi, Firenze, 1954); "Red
Woman" (*Donna rossa*) from *Sodoma e Gomorra* (Lucarini, Roma, 1991); "Empty Sky" (Untitled)
excerpted from *Io*, in *Russia e Cina* (Mondadori, Milano, 1991); "The Gun Gone Mad" (*Il fucile
impazzito*) from *Kaputt*, (Mondadori, Milano, 1979); "Sleepwalking" (Untitled) adapted from *Mamma
Marcia* (Leonardo, Milano, 1990); "Xian of Eight Rivers" (Untitled) excerpted from *Io*, in *Russia e
Cina* (Mondadori, Milano, 1991).

Library of Congress Cataloging-in-Publication Data
Malaparte, Curzio, 1898–1957.
[Works. Selections. English]
The bird that swallowed its cage : the selected writings of Curzio Malaparte / adapted and trans-
lated by Walter Murch ; with an afterword by Lawrence Weschler.
    pages cm
Includes bibliographical references and index.
ISBN 978-1-61902-281-2 pbk
1. Malaparte, Curzio, 1898-1957—Translations into English. 2. Malaparte, Curzio, 1898-1957—
Adaptations. I. Murch, Walter, 1943– II. Title.
PQ4829.A515A2 2013
858'.91209—dc23

                        2012042948

Cover painting, *Virtual Music Study #1*, © Daniele Lombardi, used by permission of the artist
Cover and interior design by Gopa & Ted2, Inc.

COUNTERPOINT
2560 Ninth Street, Suite 318
Berkeley, CA 94710
www.counterpointpress.com

Printed in the United States of America

Contents

Curzio Malaparte: Biographical Note   1

Notes on the Translations   7

That Character Called "I"   11

Murderer   21
Adapted from *Mamma Marcia*

Six Winds   37
From *Maledetti Toscani*

Two Sisters   45
From *Fughe in Prigione*

Today We Fly   53
From *Fughe in Prigione*

El Traidor   61
Excerpted from *Diario di Uno Straniero a Parigi*

The Visit of the Angel   73
From *Fughe in Prigione*

The Little Hand   81
Excerpted from *Maledetti Toscani*

PARTISANS, 1944   87
Adapted from *Mamma Marcia*

WOMAN BY THE EDGE OF THE SEA   101
From *Fughe in Prigione*

RED WOMAN   109
From *Sodoma e Gomorra*

EMPTY SKY   123
Excerpted from *Io, in Russia e Cina*

THE GUN GONE MAD   125
From *Kaputt*

SLEEPWALKING   143
Adapted from *Mamma Marcia*

XIAN OF EIGHT RIVERS   151
Excerpted from *Io, in Russia e Cina*

AFTERWORD BY LAWRENCE WESCHLER   155

The Bird That Swallowed Its Cage

Curzio Malaparte
Biographical Note

Curzio Malaparte was born in Prato, a dozen miles or so from Florence, in 1898. The contradictions and ambiguities that marked his life began immediately: he was baptized as Kurt Suckert; his father, Erwin Suckert, was a Lutheran German who had emigrated to Italy for business reasons; his mother, Evelina Perelli, was a beautiful middle-class Catholic girl from Milan. At the age of three months he was sent away to be wet-nursed, and though his mother came to visit every week, he wound up spending his first six years with the working-class family of Eugenia and Mersiade Baldi. ("The Little Hand," in this collection, gives a colorful snapshot of life with the Baldis.) When he was eventually returned to the Suckert home for schooling, his German name made him feel awkward in Italian classrooms, and he repeatedly ran away from home.

These escapes culminated at age sixteen, when he ran all the way to France to enlist in the fight against his father's native country. He served throughout the First World War, 1914–1918, rising in rank from private to lieutenant in charge of a flamethrower unit. He was hospitalized after being gassed in the Second Battle of the Marne but returned to the front and was decorated by the French for bravery. In 1919 he was given the job of director of press relations for the Versailles Peace Conference, then in 1920 he was appointed cultural attaché with the Italian embassy in Warsaw, becoming the youngest diplomat in the history of Italy.[1] It

1. Oriana Fallaci in *L'Europeo*, May 2, 1954.

was here that he had his first serious love affair (with a Polish princess), as well as his first duel—sabers at dawn with a Polish lieutenant who had maligned the conduct of Italian soldiers in the war.[2]

Malaparte returned to Italy in 1921 and launched his literary career with a controversial book, *Viva Caporetto*, excoriating the Italian generals for their conduct in the war.[3] His frustration with the status quo was broadly shared by many of his fellow veterans, and this collective urge to remake a rotten society provided kindling for the early idealistic stages of Italian fascism. Something of that youthful anger can be felt in "Murderer," the first piece in this collection.

In September 1922, Malaparte joined the PNF (National Fascist Party), and a month later, in October, Mussolini's March on Rome toppled the then-current Liberal Party government of Luigi Facta.

Even the name Malaparte, which he adopted at age twenty-seven, is ambiguous: *prendere in mala parte* means "to take offense." But is it also an ironic variation on Napoléon Bonaparte? That is the explanation Malaparte gave to his friend the journalist Lino Pellegrini: *I would have called myself Bonaparte, but the name was already taken.*[4] Or was it a fateful and psychologically apt observation about himself as the *mala parte*—the "bad part" who would never fit, or at least not for long, any of the roles that he assumed or that society assigned to him? Or was it a tacit chip-on-the-shoulder acknowledgment of the rumor, noted by Pellegrini and others, that he may not have been his father's biological child? (The similar-sounding phrase *mal partorito* means "badly born.") What is not ambiguous is that the name Malaparte is Italian and Suckert is German, and if you were a young fascist in an Italy that was reinventing itself along nationalistic lines, an Italian name would be

2. Franco Vegliani, *Malaparte* (Milan: Guarnati, 1957), 61, 62. Malaparte was victorious, wounding his opponent in the shoulder. This was the first of sixteen duels Malaparte would fight over the next thirty years.
3. The book is also known as *La Rivolta dei Santi Maledetti (The Revolt of the Cursed Saints)*. It was condemned by state censors, suppressed, and not republished until 1980.
4. Interview with Lino Pellegrini in Maurizio Serra, *Malaparte: Vies et Légendes* (Paris: Grasset, 2010), 605.

better than a German one. But as to why the specific name Malaparte was chosen, no one knows: Malaparte himself never gave a serious answer to the question.

Despite his new name, Malaparte was thrown out of the Fascist Party in 1933 and sentenced to five years in prison. One of his crimes had been writing his ninth book, *The Technique of the Coup d'État,* an exposé—published in France—of the methods used by Mussolini, Lenin, and Hitler to seize political power. Writing *Technique* was a typical Malapartian act: a provocative flourish of brilliant analysis, virtually challenging Mussolini, with whom he was on speaking but not on intimate terms, to act against him. Which, unsurprisingly, Mussolini did. The book was banned in Italy and burned in Germany.

Mug shots of Malaparte upon his arrest by Mussolini in 1933.

His other crime was to have written unflatteringly about Italo Balbo, the head of Italy's air force and Mussolini's heir apparent. For this, Malaparte was accused, variously, of "having carried out anti-fascist activities while abroad," "slander and defamation of a Minister in charge," and failing to be "faithful to his oath."[5]

Malaparte was in Scotland when he decided to return to Italy, and something of his fatalistic mood can be judged from "Woman by the Edge of the Sea," also in this collection. The experience of rejection

5. Giordano Bruno Guerri, *L'Arcitaliano: Vita di Curzio Malaparte* (Milan: Bompiani, 1980), 150–51.

and imprisonment at age thirty-five, after a brilliant and successful youth, brought him up short, affecting him deeply and permanently.

After two months of suspense in cell 461 of Regina Coeli prison, he learned that his sentence was being moderated to exile on the islands of Lipari, then Ischia, and subsequently to house arrest in Forte dei Marmi, on the mainland.

Cell 461 remains in my soul as its secret character, he wrote in the 1943 introduction to *Fughe in Prigione:*

> *The cell is within me like a child inside a pregnant woman.*
> *I am a bird that has swallowed its cage.*

His sentence was lifted prematurely in 1935 through the intervention of Galeazzo Ciano (Mussolini's son-in-law), and Malaparte was allowed to resume his literary activities. There must have been something about the island isolation, however, that agreed with him: he used his freedom to design and construct Casa Malaparte, a severely modern/ancient cell block with windows on another island, Capri, at the tip of a remote promontory accessible only by sea or by a long walk along a rocky trail. He rejected the original plans by Adalberto Libera and instead designed and built the house with the help of Alfonso Amitrano, a local mason. It was:

> *a melancholy, austere house which I have built on a solitary cliff by the sea. A house which is the ghost, the secret image, of prison. Perhaps I never really wanted—not even when I was inside—to break out of jail. The destiny of man is not to live in freedom, but to live free within a prison.*[6]

Casa Malaparte occupies a unique place in twentieth-century domestic architecture. Several books have been dedicated to studying

6. Also from the introduction to the 1943 edition of *Fughe in Prigione.* Translation by Walter Murch.

and celebrating it,[7] and it was used by Jean-Luc Godard as a central location for *Contempt* (1963), starring Brigitte Bardot, Jack Palance, and Fritz Lang.

When the Second World War broke out, Malaparte was made a captain in the reserves and sent far away to the eastern and northern fronts—the Ukraine and Finland—as a war correspondent for *Corriere della Sera*, presumably to get him out of domestic circulation and into harm's way. If so, the plan backfired: Malaparte not only survived to write provocative columns challenging the expectation of Russian defeat, but used the opportunity to write his masterpiece, *Kaputt* (1944), a powerfully styled, five-hundred-page amalgam of his wartime experiences that quickly became an international best-seller.

He returned to Italy after Mussolini's fall and, following a few more sojourns in jail, began working as a liaison officer between the occupying Allied forces and the Italian Liberation army. Another memoir, *The Skin* (1949)—condemned by the Catholic Church—emerged from this experience and was almost as well received as *Kaputt*. A film version of *The Skin* was made in 1981 by Liliana Cavani, starring Marcello Mastroianni as Malaparte.

His political sympathies after the war turned to communism, a viable political stance in Italy at the time, but, given Malaparte's fascist past, this aroused suspicion on both sides of the country's postwar literary and political climate.

Emigrating to France in 1947, he wrote two plays (in French) that were produced the following year: *Du Côté de Chez Proust* and *Das Kapital*. They met with little success—their literary presumption roiled the critics—and he left Paris soon after, to try his luck with *Il Cristo Proibito* (*Forbidden Christ*, also known as *Strange Deception*), a film he wrote and directed, and for which he composed the music. Its subject was postwar retribution and reconciliation, and though it won the City of Berlin prize at the first Berlin Film Festival, in 1951, and was one of

---

7. See *Malaparte: A House Like Me*, by the architect Michael McDonough (New York: Clarkson Potter, 1999).

the National Board of Review's top five foreign films of the year, it was not a commercial success.

Malaparte had returned Italy in 1949 to write and shoot the film, and he stayed on afterward, directing an opera *(La Fanciulla del West)* and writing books, a play, newspaper columns, and even a musical revue, *Sexophone*, with him as grease-painted master of ceremonies.

In October 1956 he embarked on a four-month trip to Russia and China—he was one of the first Westerners to interview Mao Zedong after the Korean War—and it was in China that he learned of the lung cancer that would soon take his life. He died in a Roman hospital in July 1957, but not before getting his membership card in the Italian Communist Party and then, perhaps, converting to Catholicism (there is a controversy about this). He is buried according to his wishes on a hill in Tuscany, overlooking his birthplace, Prato.

He never married, though there were many women in his life—the pseudonymous Lavinias, Flaminias, and Tanias who appear throughout his work and who are the central focus of three of the stories in this collection: *The Visit of the Angel*, *Woman by the Edge of the Sea*, and *Red Woman*.

Today, the problematic contradictions and collisions of Malaparte's life seem like a sped-up film of the first half of the twentieth century: German-Italian, Protestant-Catholic, fascist-communist, journalist-novelist, editor-architect, playwright-columnist, film director-composer, soldier-pacifist, diplomat-prisoner. Almost sixty years after his death, he remains a controversial, polarizing figure in Italy.

Notes on the Translations

I knew nothing about Malaparte until a fortuitous encounter in France in 1986. I was in Lyon at the time, working as film editor on Philip Kaufman's *The Unbearable Lightness of Being*, and had run out of things to read. A bookstore down the street filled the gap with Hubert Reeves's *L'Heure de s'enivrer*, a book about cosmology. And somewhere in its middle pages, to illustrate a point about conditions shortly after the Big Bang, the author retold a fragment of one of Malaparte's stories. Its imagery was so strange and compelling—a stampede of horses flash-frozen in Russia's Lake Ladoga during the siege of Leningrad—that I determined to find the book from which the story was taken: it turned out to be *Kaputt*.

It would be difficult to overestimate the effect *Kaputt* had on me: reading it was like falling into a dream—or nightmare—tenuously balanced on the tightrope between real and surreal. There is also throughout the book a feeling of deeply bruised, almost curdled idealism, where pessimism about the human condition is somewhat relieved with the narcotic of irony and flashes of what the French call *l'humour implacable*. In his captain's uniform, with his literary prestige and *vieux enfant terrible* persona, Malaparte had managed to get very close to the radioactive core of the Axis powers, and the book's revelations about the inner workings, personalities, and experiences on the "other side" is like a report from the interior of a social-political Chernobyl. I couldn't understand why I hadn't heard of Malaparte before, nor why

Kaputt wasn't on a required reading list for every citizen of the twentieth century.

I bought a dozen copies to give to my friends, anticipating an explosion of interest. The result was instead a little smoke—perhaps a flame or two—but lots of shrugs and raised eyebrows. I read the two other books by Malaparte that have been translated into English: *The Volga Rises in Europe* (1943) and *The Skin* (1949). I resumed my study of Italian, which I had let lapse after 1964, and asked friends in Italy to send me books of Malaparte's that were unobtainable in the USA: *Fughe in Prigione, Maledetti Toscani, Mamma Marcia*, and others.

But my interest never extended to translation. At least not until 1997, after I had been interviewed by the poetry journal *Parnassus* on the subject of film adaptation and *The English Patient*. In the course of my conversation with the interviewer, Joy Katz, I offered an analogy: that filmmakers adapting a novel are performing a kind of multilevel translation from the language of text to the languages of image, movement, and sound, and that the old Italian adage *traduttore, traditore* (translator, traitor) particularly applies: an attempt to be overly faithful to the text often results in a damming-up of its deeper currents, so that an artful betrayal of the original work seems to serve an adaptation best, something along the lines of Picasso's dictum: *art is a lie that tells the truth.*

After finishing the interview, however, I suddenly realized that I didn't really know what I was talking about, at least as far as any personal experience of language translation was concerned. So I decided to try it—and what better subject than Malaparte?

I was relieved to find that the process felt familiar, with the right blend of challenge and discovery, but I was surprised that some of the translations of Malaparte's prose seemed to want to arrange themselves in short lines of free verse. This was particularly mysterious to me because I am what might charitably be called "poetically challenged." I love poetry in the abstract but have a blind spot for most poems in particular, somewhat like those unfortunate people who love humanity but have a hard time with human beings. Although there were some exceptions—I had long appreciated Rilke and Dickinson, for instance—my poetic "tone deafness" bothered me and I was eager to see where this experiment might lead.

Over the years, I worked on a number of Malaparte's stories and meditations, none of which had yet been translated into English. Many of them, like the first, wound up also being "translated" from prose into free-verse format. With hindsight, there appear to be four reasons for this shift: the rich, almost overwhelming density of Malaparte's original text; the fabulous nature of his imagery; his frequent use of repetitions and chantlike sequences *(dented wheels, transmission belts, gleaming steel handles, bearings, gauges, gearings, and crankshafts scattered on the factory floor)*; and the cross-sensory nature of his metaphors *(the air filled with water and stone; a bitter blue light).*

Allowing more space on the page also seemed to aerate the density of Malaparte's text, allowing it to breathe and permitting his startling images to be savored in a more measured way. And since Italian—particularly Malaparte's Italian—is a more sonorous language than English, the poetic form helped to restore some of the musicality and rhythm lost in a prose translation.

In the process, I also rediscovered the obvious, which is that the ragged structure of free verse emphasizes the internal rhythms and tensions of each line and puts an added, though subliminal, emphasis on the line's last word, an emphasis that is independent of the grammatical construction of the sentence. This explained the familiarity I had felt earlier: translating in this way turned out to be closely similar to film editing and sound design, which are my principal occupations.

Rhythm, both internal to the shot (or line) and then in the sequence of shots (or lines), is of course as central to film editing as it is to poetry. Once a shot is selected, the crucial decision becomes *at what precise moment* to bring it to an end, even though this decision is perceived only subliminally by the audience. Just as the end of a line in free verse is usually independent of the grammatical structure of the sentence, the end of a shot in a film is usually independent of the overall dramatic structure of a scene. But in both cases, the ending of a line (or shot) is a seemingly arbitrary but secretly architectural way for the creators to shape the arc of the poem or story, largely by drawing subtle comparison and contrasts between the final image of the outgoing shot and the first image of the next.

There are also the larger questions common to translation and film editing: when to follow the text or the script literally; when to eliminate; when to augment or repeat; when to transpose; when to invent. Once the technical issues have been mastered, these become the dominant questions in the postproduction of a film.

And then there was an added bonus: I found that the immediacy of language translation helped to solve—for me, anyway—a persistent practical dilemma in the life of every film editor: there is usually no way to edit, in a fully creative sense, without actually *working on a film*. It is as if a musician found he could perform only in official full-dress concerts, without the ability to practice on his own or in smaller groups. The resonances between film editing and translation provided me with an alternate "cross-training" that is so important in the lives of artists and athletes, but that is generally denied to most filmmakers because of the technical and expensive nature of our particular crafts.

That Character Called "I"

In early June of 1944, Malaparte had momentarily joined up with the French Expeditionary Forces—Moroccan troops known as *goumiers*—under the command of a General Guillaume. They were all waiting for the American Fifth Army tank divisions on their way north to occupy Rome. As he relates the following incident in *The Skin*, Malaparte, his friend Colonel Jack Hamilton,[8] and the French officers were having lunch alfresco, while the officers were gently teasing Malaparte about the uncanny ability he seemed to possess, in *Kaputt*, for somehow always managing to witness the most incredible events.

> *You won't ask us to believe,* said Pierre Lyautey, *that all that Malaparte relates in* Kaputt *actually happened to him? Is it really possible that everything happens to* him? *Nothing ever happens to* me.
>
> *I would not wish to be discourteous to Malaparte, for he is my guest,* said General Guillaume, *but I think that in* Kaputt *he is pulling his readers' legs.*

General Guillaume and Pierre Lyautey were not alone in their doubts about Malaparte's writing: many readers over the years have

---

8. Colonel Jack Hamilton in *The Skin* was in reality Col. Henry H. Cumming, U.S. Army. The French officers' names are historically correct.

Curzio Malaparte in 1946.

wondered the same thing. In this case, as we will see, Malaparte even places the question of his own reliability at the very center of the story. But for the moment, he endures their teasing in silence, allowing Hamilton to rise to his defense:

> *What does it matter,* said Jack, *whether what Malaparte tells us is true or false? What matters is how he tells it.*

Meanwhile, somewhere in the background, a German booby trap blows off the hand of an unfortunate *goumier*. The lengthy luncheon proceeds unimpeded through several other courses, along with more teasing, finally capped by the main dish—a plate of Moroccan lamb couscous. The French commanders speculate about how this meal will be described in Malaparte's next book: perhaps it will be set not on farm tables among oak trees, but at the pope's nearby Castel Gandolfo, with a heavenly chorus for musical accompaniment.

Malaparte is finally roused to speak:

Please forgive me, I said at last, turning to General Guillaume,
*if I am forced to reveal to you that a few moments ago, at this very
table, I had the most extraordinary experience of my life.*

He then scandalizes these battle-hardened soldiers, revealing to them
that as they were teasing him he had been coolly eating the amputated
hand of the unfortunate *goumier,* it had landed in the kettle of couscous
and been inadvertently served up to him. Being well-mannered and
not wishing to upset the convivial mood, he had forced himself not
to cry out, and:

*I calmly began eating the hand. The flesh was a little tough. It had
not had time to cook.*
Taisez-vous! cried General Guillaume in a hoarse voice,
pushing away the plate that lay in front of him. They all looked
appalled, and were staring at me with wide-open eyes.

Whether Guillaume was horrified that Malaparte would actually
commit such an act or simply that he would have the gall to invent
this story of couscous cannibalism, it is worth keeping in mind that
Malaparte's reputation was already sufficiently diabolical (as Malaparte
well knew) to give his story traction among these cultured officers. He
then cements his reputation by showing them the bones of the *goumier's*
hand, carefully arranged on his plate, along with the five fingernails.

*You will forgive me if, in spite of my good breeding, I wasn't equal
to swallowing the nails.*
Mon Dieu! cried General Guillaume, gulping down a glass
of wine at a single draught.

The moment is interrupted by a distant cannon shot from a Sherman
tank—the arrival of the American Fifth Army—and everyone scatters

to take up positions. Hamilton and Malaparte run down the hill to their jeep, laughing at Malaparte's "joke."

> *That will teach them to question the truth of what you say in* Kaputt! cried Jack as he ran.
> *Did you see how carefully I arranged those lamb bones on my plate? They looked just like the bones of a hand.*
> And we roared with laughter as we ran among the trees.

Almost everywhere in Malaparte's work, the narrator is "I"—or, as he once described it, *that character called "I."*[9] The presence of this first-person voice intensifies the force field surrounding the sequence of events, particularly since those events often have a fabulous penumbral glow that makes us wonder, along with Lyautey and Guillaume: can all this really be true? The writing is of such a caliber that we *want* to believe the strange, awful, beautiful, horrible things in Malaparte's books, and that Malaparte was actually there to witness them—a Dante traveling through this Inferno. Had *Kaputt* been written in the third person, the French officers would probably have tacitly accepted the book as invented literature. But *Kaputt* and *The Skin*, as well as many of the stories in this collection, have the sheen of first-person "I was there" journalism, and so the question of their veracity inevitably arises.

In the story of the *goumier's* hand, Malaparte slyly mocks the officers for their craving to know the objective truth. He implies that they, as warriors, should know—more than anyone—that war is full of the most incredible, tragic, surreal events, and to write a book about war, especially this war, without capturing that tragic surreality, is to miss the target.

And yet . . . a deeper problem lies hidden within this story: when the French were serving couscous alfresco and teasing Malaparte about *Kaputt, Kaputt* had not yet been published. Malaparte had written most of the manuscript in 1941–1943, but he was still making revisions in the

9. From Malaparte's introduction to his *Journal d'un Étranger à Paris* (Paris: Denoël, 1967).

spring of 1944, and the book wasn't finally published until October.[10] How, then, could the French officers have been familiar with it at the beginning of June?

The answer is: they couldn't.

So then why would Malaparte insinuate this extra twist into a story that already turns on the question of his own reliability? In his introduction to *Kaputt,* Malaparte claims that he finished the manuscript in September 1943, and in his introduction to the French edition of *The Skin,* he writes that *Kaputt* was published *shortly after the Allied landing in 1943.*[11] We can't be sure of his motives for this fudge, but an earlier publication date would credit him with anticipating, even provoking, the surge of antifascist sentiment, rather than seeming to ride its coattails.[12]

With the foregoing in mind, it is worth taking a look at the "I" voice in *Partisans,* the eighth story in this collection. The narrator here is indistinguishable from the narrator of *The Skin,* and the events in *Partisans* are just as vividly observed. But if we are searching for journalistic truth, we have to choose between the two stories because their narrators are in different parts of the world on the same date: June 4, 1944, when American tanks drove through the gates of Rome. One "I" was in Italy having couscous with the French Expeditionary Forces; the other "I" was in Finland:

> It was the end of June, 1944: midsummer in the Arctic. I turned on the radio—every day brought more battles, more bombardments, more massacres. As soon as I snapped off the

10. *Kaputt* was published by Gaspare Casella, in Naples, in October 1944 (Serra, *Malaparte: Vies et Légendes,* 346). From September 1943, Italy was divided in half between opposing armies and virtually in a state of civil war for twenty months, until the final defeat of the German forces in May 1945. Getting any book published under these circumstances is a remarkable achievement.

11. "*Lettre à mes Camarades Français de 1914–1918,*" the introduction to *La Peau,* the French translation of *La Pelle,* published by Denoël in 1949.

12. Much of Malaparte's *Diario di Uno Straniero a Parigi,* written in 1948, published posthumously in 1966, is concerned with defending himself against the accusation of being a collaborator with the fascist cause during the war.

switch, the horrendous smell of blood hovering over Europe
began to dissipate. And the silence, the splendid purity of the
Nordic summer, started to gain the upper hand.

Svarstrom came in to where I was resting and announced:
They have taken Rome.

Je m'en fous. I couldn't care less.

It's your country, said Svarstrom.

Je m'en fous.

Don't you care who has taken Rome? asked Svarstrom.

No.

*It was the Allies. They entered Rome last night. The pope blessed
the Allied army from the loggia of St. Peter's.*

Je m'en fous.

We know that Malaparte was working as a liaison officer somewhere
near Rome on June 4, 1944, so the "I" of *Partisans* cannot be him.
Instead, it is Malaparte imagining how things might have been if he
had remained in Finland after the fall of Mussolini. So should the story
be dismissed as a fabrication? The answer is not that simple. First of
all, *Mamma Marcia*—the book from which *Partisans* is excerpted—was
published posthumously, so we can never be sure what changes Malaparte might have made if he had lived. More significantly, the identity
of the narrator of *Partisans* is never revealed: he is simply "I"—*this
character called "I"*—someone who is identified as Italian, and who has
many of Malaparte's personality traits. But the actual name Malaparte
never appears in *Partisans*.

On one level, then, *Partisans* is an imagined reality. Yet Malaparte
had been in Finland throughout much of 1942–1943, and some version
of the events in the story, concerning the amputation of a gangrenous
leg, may have happened, and Malaparte may have witnessed them:
there is a specificity to the writing that is undeniably compelling. It is
a story, then, phrased in a journalistic, first-person present but operating
as a meditation on the psychology of corruption and defeat, set in the
splendid purity of the Nordic summer, far from Italy, detached physically

and spiritually from the hot and grimy events of the actual defeat itself, in a world where the narrator has the luxury of saying *Je m'en fous,* a world that is

> *a reflection of a universe far from us,*
> *a universe foreign to us, inhuman,*
> *a universe of cruel and impassive abstraction.*

Questions concerning the relationship between an author's life and work may be routine, but they are inevitable when it comes to Malaparte: Should his work be calibrated with reference to his life, or separately? Was his work a reflection of his life, or a refuge from it? Or both? These are difficult questions under any circumstances, but particularly so with Malaparte, since his life was so extraordinary and his writing so seemingly autobiographical.

Arthur Koestler, a similarly controversial and "engaged" author a few years younger than Malaparte, acknowledged these complexities with his observation that *meeting an author after reading his work is like meeting the goose after eating the pâté.*

So, a cautionary note: the "I" in these stories is mutable, and its authenticity is further complicated by Malaparte's stature during his lifetime as a high-profile, sometimes opportunistic, deliberately pro-vocative intellectual chameleon, who on the other hand was apparently reserved in private life, acutely sensitive to shades of meaning, and monastic in his dedication to the written word.[13]

As you read this material, then, be aware that there is often an artfully concealed borderland between the objective truths, of which there are many, and the deeper truths of subjectivity masquerading as objectivity, which are the more significant.

The selection of material in this collection, spanning more than twenty-five years of Malaparte's writing, is my own.

---

13. Interview with Lino Pellegrini in Serra, *Malaparte: Vies et Légendes,* 608–609.

The versions of *Murderer, Partisans,* and *The Gun Gone Mad* presented here are unusual in that they mix prose and free verse, a combination that arose spontaneously during translation. All three are stories of wartime, shifting stylistically between action and contemplation, and it was this alternation that prompted the difference in format.

Murderer, Partisans, and *Sleepwalking* were untitled and unfinished at the time of Malaparte's death. Their present endings are not invented, however, but created by the restructuring of existing material until the arrangement seemed to arrive at a resolution.

Those three titles are my suggestions, as are *Empty Sky, The Little Hand, El Traidor,* and *Six Winds,* which were also untitled in the originals.

There is no way of knowing what Malaparte would think of all this, but I hope that he would approve, or at least be intrigued, given the multiplicity of the creative forms he deployed, the languages he spoke fluently, and the variety of roles he played throughout the first half of the contentious century just ended.

Walter Murch
February, 2012
Bolinas, California

È certo assai più difficile perdere una guerra che vincerla. A vincere una guerra tutti son buoni, non tutti son capaci di perderla.

It is certainly harder to lose a war than to win one. Everyone is capable of winning a war, not everyone is capable of losing one.

—CURZIO MALAPARTE, *The Skin*, 1949

Murderer

A Narrative in Four Scenes and Six Songs

(1959)

Malaparte ran away from school in Tuscany at the start of the
First World War, when he was sixteen. He lied about his age to join
the Légion Garibaldienne, a volunteer brigade of Italians fighting
alongside the French against the Germans. When Italy entered
the war in 1915, he joined the regular army. During the four years
of combat he rose from private to the rank of lieutenant.

In the late 1940s he returned home to Tuscany to attend to
his dying mother.

I

The whole of human history . . .

> The whole of human history
> seems to be the story of men who kill,
> and of men who are killed;
> of murderers who light their cigarettes
> with trembling hands,
> and of poor, unlucky kids staring into the eyes
> of those who bring them their deaths.

But history is not about murderers, after all.
It is just the story of some poor kids.
The whole history of the world
is just the story of millions of poor kids
overwhelmed by the fear of death, or
by the fear of bringing death to others.

My mother had closed her eyes
and was breathing softly.
Every so often, her right hand,
abandoned on the white sheet,
would shift slightly, opening and closing
like the hand of a sleeping baby.

The nurse came into the room just then,
as I had begun to tell the story of Jaco.
She opened the door as slowly as possible,
but I felt her presence behind my shoulders
bending over the bed,
looking at my mother.

She is sleeping, said the nurse.
Don't wake her.

I didn't turn around,
but continued my story in a low whisper.
When I got to the part about the grenade,
I heard the nurse tiptoeing out,
closing the door behind her,

silently.

The grenade exploded a few feet away, while Jaco was helping to carry two wounded soldiers down the hill to the hospital tent. By the time I got to him, he was stretched out on the grass, breathing heavily. Everyone around him had been killed. He watched as I approached, and when I was close, he smiled.

He had just been promoted lieutenant, even though he had not yet turned nineteen. Six months ago, when we were getting ready to leave Italy, Ercolani had taken me aside and said: *Look out for Jaco. He's like a brother to me. Make sure nothing bad happens to him.*

I was irritated: *War isn't a game. It doesn't play by the rules. If something bad happens to him, tough luck.*

But from that day on, I kept my eye on Jacoboni: he was about the same age as me, but seemed much younger. In any event, he turned out to be a good officer: he did his duty like all the others, like a good kid. He took war seriously, convinced he would go home in one piece, back to his family in Monterotondo, near Rome. And it was perhaps because of this that he smiled as I sat down next to him.

I saw right away that it was hopeless. The grenade had torn open his abdomen and his intestines were cascading down his leg past his knees and coiling onto the ground.

We were surrounded by the dead: hundreds of them in the forest around us. Most were Italian, but there were a few Germans: they had advanced this far before we had finally pushed them back. Their dead lay alongside ours.

It began to rain.

> The rain on the oak leaves
> made a soft music, like women whispering.
> Every so often, it would intensify
> as it darted here and there through the trees,
> rising and then fading away.

The green reflections of the forest
washed everything the color of water,
gave an extraordinary lightness to things:
to the solid trunks of the trees,
to the bodies lying in the grass.

Glimpsed through the branches of the trees,
the sky appeared light and remote:
A sky made of silk,
luminous and pure, serene,
scrubbed of clouds and fog.

The rain was coming from who knows where.
Or maybe it was not even rain,
just the memory of some rain
falling from the depths of past summers,
falling from some childhood summer long ago.

II

The soldiers under Jaco's command ran over to see what had happened
to him, and from my expression they understood there was nothing
to be done. Finally, one of them turned and drifted away, followed by
the rest. Every so often they glanced back over their shoulders. I felt as
if they were looking not at poor Jaco, but at me. When I finally stood
up and also started to move away, Jaco asked me to stay: *Don't leave me
alone* . . . I sat back down on the grass next to him and called out to the
other soldiers: *Come back! Don't leave him alone.* They were Jacoboni's
soldiers, after all, not mine.

They returned and sat down on the grass in a circle around Jaco.
There was a long silence. Every so often, coming from somewhere deep
in the woods, we would hear a metallic scraping and then the sound

of rough voices—that indistinct noise soldiers make when they are preparing to attack. Jaco's soldiers began polishing their rifles using the oil from a tin of sardines. We had only one machine gun that worked, a Fiat, but no water for its cooling jacket, so a sergeant held the gun steady and some of the soldiers pissed into it.

We were like wild animals in the woods, wounded animals who hear the hunt closing in: the hurried panting of the dogs and the voices of the hunters, those green voices in the yellow-green air of the woods.

It was unbearable...

The morning was sweet, fresh, transparent.
The rain lit up the trunks of the trees
as it does in certain French paintings.
Lit up the grass, too, which from a dark green
around the trees slowly lightened
as it edged out into the open,
only to darken again further on
as it neared another grove.
We heard the hidden presence all around us
of terrified hare, pheasant, rabbit,
of deer crouched in some hole among the bushes.

The sky above shone pure, serene,
with a trace of blue so delicate it was almost green,
and the even-deeper green of the woods all around
was light and transparent,
full of birdsong.

But on the rosy dawn of Jaco's face
the grey shadow of his evening
was slowly lengthening—
as if the sun, having not yet reached the summit
of its crimson arc, was already setting,

melting, pure and delicate,
into the peaceful blue of the sky,
into a motionless brilliance
flaming the tips of the trees, the grass,
the fragrant fields of wheat.

The dazzling incandescence of that day,
of that summer morning rich with the smell of grass,
of leaves, of invisible waters,
rich with the fresh smell of rain,
the light of that morning was a brilliant shadow
veiling the glare of the sun
such that the trees,
reflecting the light from one another,
from trunk to trunk
from bough to bough,
had reformed themselves in the mirrored water of a pool
into an upside-down perspective
where I saw white clouds floating in the grass,
like water lilies.

But little by little Jacoboni's face was fading away,
that grey shadow was slowly descending
onto his poor child's face
from a remote impirium
full of delicate and dazzling light.

I can't take it any more,
he whispered, fixing each of us, one by one,
with his gaze, smiling, and silently moving his lips.

Then he began to struggle.
He struggled, grinding his teeth.
He struggled like a wounded animal,

silently, holding us in his gaze.
His eyes, his smile, his childlike expression
were exactly those of a dog in agony,
a dying dog, who looks to his master for relief.

We could do nothing to ease his suffering,
And so we all kept silent.
But within each of us something
had begun to move,
to be born.

It was just then that one of the girls began to scream.

III

There were three of them—three prostitutes: young, lighthearted, courageous—recently arrived on foot from Épernay. To save themselves during the battle they had jumped into a trench some yards away. They had been there for two days now, huddled down, and every so often we would hear them cry out, weeping. A week or so earlier, a delegation from the *maréchaussée* had warned all the Allied soldiers—French, English, Italian, American, Senegalese, Annamite, Belgian, Portuguese—not to fraternize with any prostitutes who might be making their way to the front.

The three girls were peasants, probably from Burgundy. They said that they had walked all the way from Troyes trying to reach Chateau Thierry, where they had heard the Americans were garrisoned. At Épernay they had found the road blocked by the *maréchaussée*, so they had taken the route which crossed the mountains as it wound its way up from Épernay through Nanteuil-la-Fosse and then down to Reims itself. Frightened by the noise of the heavy artillery which was bom-

barding the road around Reims, they had veered off from Nanteuil-la-
Fosse into the Ardre Valley and eventually wound up here in the Bois
de Corton a few hours before the beginning of the offensive.

I was told about them during the night.

There are three girls, said Sergeant Rossi, beaming.

Beautiful?

Beautiful enough.

Where are they?

Over there.

We have to send them back.

Right now? How can we?

*Post a sentry with them and make sure no one gets close. We'll consign them
over to the* maréchaussée *when the attack is finished.*

Sergeant Rossi moved off in silence, turning to look back at me
with a strange expression.

A little later, I went to see where the girls were. I found the sentry
at his post, sitting on the grass with his rifle between his legs. But the
girls were not there.

Where have they gone? I said.

*Sergeant Rossi came and took one of them away. The other two went look-
ing for the kitchens.*

I eventually found those two in a trench, disheveled and dirty, surrounded by a group of soldiers staring down in silence, eyes narrowed
to slits. The girls looked like beasts huddled in their lair. When I arrived,
one of them was crouched down with her skirts raised, her face red
from the effort of defecating. I crept up slowly, in silence, and none of
the soldiers noticed. But the girl was now looking at me, frightened.
The soldiers kept staring at her in their slit-eyed silence. When I got
closer, she stood up, lowered her skirts, and then remained standing,
looking at me timidly.

Bonjour, monsieur l'officier, she said, trembling.

At this, all of the soldiers turned around and stood up, ashamed. But I
knew they were furious, that at that moment they hated me. The other
girl, sitting in a corner of the trench, put one hand over a breast while
adjusting her dress to cover her knees with the other.

She also greeted me: *Bonjour, monsieur.*

What are you doing? I said to the soldiers. *You're not even letting her do her business. Take off!*

She does it anyway, said one of the soldiers. *Every so often she crouches down and does her business.*

She has diarrhea, said another.

No, she's doing it on purpose, said a third, and in his empty eyes I saw the flickering of an oil lamp.

Take off, I said. *It isn't right for you to be here, looking at them like this. After all, they are two women.*

They're just two whores, said a soldier. *It's not our fault if that's the way they are.*

We are all a bunch of whores, I said. *If we weren't, we wouldn't be here in these woods, waiting to be wiped out like rats.*

It's true, said the soldiers. *The lieutenant is right. We're all a bunch of whores.*

Someone laughed. But most of them remained silent, looking at me. One of the two girls began to cry, then screamed: *I want to leave, I want to get out of here; I'm scared!* The scream, more than the tears, woke something in the soldiers that at first seemed to be a kind of gaiety, but was instead hate, anger, and fear all mixed together with disgust.

You're in it now, they laughed, *up to your necks! You wanted to come here? To make love? You're going to die like the rest of us. You want to go back home? So do we. But it doesn't matter, we're all going to die anyway.*

Suddenly one of the soldiers began to urinate into the trench, and then another, and then all of them, standing around the trench urinating on the two girls. And they laughed, but with anger and hate, and they shook their penises, spraying the urine in every direction, soaking the two girls. I shouted *Stop!* and hit one of them, accidentally knocking him into the trench. The rest screamed with laughter and urinated even more wildly, but it was laughter tinged with hate, colored by the strange accents with which hate stains the voice:

You want to go home, too? You don't want to die? You're a whore who just wants to go home, like them. You thought you'd come here and make love? You're going to die like the rest of us, you stupid whore!

And so they kept on urinating into the trench, on their comrade and the two girls, shaking their swollen, hairy penises. I shouted: *Stop!*

But they were too far gone...

There were all those dead in the grass around us,
in the woods. All those dead from yesterday,
from the night before, from the morning,
already beginning to stink.
There were all those dead,
our dead comrades, all around us.
And the soldiers knew that, like them,
they too must die, gripped
by that delirium
which descends out of the blue
when men know that they must die.

It wasn't their fault
if generals, ministers, kings, and emperors,
if presidents of republics, heads of steelworks,
bankers, and actresses singing the Marseillaise
draped in the flag,
forgot that before soldiers were soldiers
soldiers had been men.

It wasn't their fault
if generals, ministers, *grands seigneurs,*
all ordered them to *Shut up!*
It wasn't their fault
if they were not thought to be men,
but only soldiers; not human beings,
but only beasts condemned to die
for the gruesome scarecrows
of Glory and Fatherland,

and for Liberty—
They who are slaves;
and for The Future of the World—
They who will die tomorrow,
They who have only the future of a day,
A night, an hour, a minute, an instant.

At the moment, though, they were men
abandoning themselves to instinct,
to the joys of being men, pissing
on everything that reminded them of their condition,
on their enslavement, on their humiliation;
on everything that makes a human being
miserable and unhappy.

It would have been easy for me to snap them to attention by simply commanding *Shut up!* But for two years now I had also been a soldier, and I knew that a soldier's deepest wish was to be a man, to return to being a man, to prove to himself—if only for an instant—that he was still capable of being a man. For two years now I also had lived under sentence of death and been told to *Shut up!* by everyone: generals, ministers, bankers, captains. And so now I found I could not in turn shout *Shut up!* at these men. I was not a general, or a banker, or a minister, or even an actress from the Comédie-Française. I was a nineteen-year-old lieutenant unable to bring himself to shout at these men, many of whom were so much older than me—thirty, thirty-five, thirty-eight. Some of them could have been my father.

And then, also, I felt as they did.

I also would have liked to piss on the world, on the generals, the ministers, the bankers, on that soldier, on those two girls; on those false fronts of Glory, of Fatherland, of Liberty, of the Future, of Progress, of Civilization. I also would have liked to piss wildly, penis in hand, on everything around: on France, Italy, England, Germany, Russia, on everyone's fatherland, mine and everyone else's, on the whole forsaken race of men, to soak wildly all the cowards and bastards who had ever yelled at us: *Shut up!*

But just at that moment the sky ripped open with the screech and crash of a grenade. Everyone fell silent. The soldiers pulled up their pants and turned around: a man was running in our direction, screaming. He had a head wound, and passed close by without noticing us, still screaming. He zigzagged into the woods, groping desperately like the blind, until he ran full tilt against a tree and fell backward on the ground, immobile.

IV

So it did not come as a surprise—a relief, almost—when we heard the *tac-tac-tac* of machine guns and the thud of grenades rising up from the woods below. The Germans were advancing again through the tangle of bomb-shattered branches, clearing a path with axe-blows, foreheads crushed beneath the overhang of great steel helmets, gleaming eyes fixed dead ahead.

The rest of that day was bitter, and many of us fell forever headlong in the grass. But toward evening the voice of battle began to diminish, and then from the depths of the forest we could hear the song of the wounded: the serene, monotonous, sad-hopeful song of the wounded, joining the chorus of birds hidden in the foliage as they welcomed the return of the moon.

It was still daylight, but the moon was rising sweetly from behind the forested mountains of Reims.

It was green against a white and tender sky . . .

> A moon from the forest of Ardennes,
> a moon from the country of Rimbaud, of Verlaine,
> a delicate green moon, round and light,

entering the room of the sky from behind a screen of branches
as if stepping delicately out of the earth,
rising up from the grass, causing the tree-branches to blush
transparent and sweet.

Like startled birds, we had settled again around Jaco:
I can't stand it any more, he smiled.
Don't let me suffer.
But now his smile was tired:
a tired smile
in a face clenched like a fist.

Jaco's suffering gnawed away at us,
sinking into our bones.
There is nothing so terrible, or so sweet,
so touching, as that animal, man,
when he gives over to death.
I felt my shirt sticking to my back. My face
and the faces of the others were beaded with sweat,
like the sweet face of Nazzareno Jacoboni.
And little by little I became aware
that everyone had slowly turned toward me,
pinning me down with their eyes.

Along with Jaco's terrible, unbearable suffering,
something else was sinking into us, little by little,
something which was not ours.
Something strong, strange, insistent,
was slowly being born within us.
Jaco stared at me,
even he now stared at me,
expecting something,
and I felt a new idea forming inside me,
and inside the others.

I can't go on, said Jaco.
I looked away to the green moon hanging behind the trees:
It had taken on the round shapeliness
of a fragrant leaf: a laurel leaf,
perhaps, or sage, or mint,
a great green leaf, transparent with evening daylight.
The sun had not yet settled into the forest,
and his last warm rays struck the trunks of the trees
leaving some of them wounded, bleeding.
Others—the oaks, the beeches, poplars and birches—
reflected the light in a strange way,
as if they were made of glass.

That glassy light, which the sun, just before it sets,
draws from the earth's waters,
drinks from its grass, from its leaves,
from the trunks of its trees,
to slake its thirst.

All of them stared at me,
but I was not aware of what I was doing.
I felt my hands moving,
but I did not know what I was doing until
I found myself standing
and saw them looking up at me,
and Jacoboni smiling at me strangely,
and felt something cold and smooth in my hands.

And finally I was aware that I was standing
with a rifle in my hands.
I closed my eyes, and fired.
I fired with my eyes closed,
one shot after another.

And then, when the echo of the shots
had melted into the woods,
there was a great silence.

With my eyes still closed,
rifle still in hand,
I turned and took a few steps.
Suddenly I heard: *Murderer! Murderer!*

It was the voice of a woman, terrible,
the voice of a sister, desperate,
the voice of a mother, of a lover.
And at that moment nothing could have been more terrible
than that voice of a woman,
that voice of a mother, of a sister,
of a lover, crying:

Murderer!

I opened my eyes and saw one of the girls running toward me, her
hands like claws, as if she intended to tear me apart. She screamed again:
Murderer! and then stopped abruptly a few paces away, filthy, disheveled,
with a great bewilderment spreading across her face, a wondrous pity.
I stood in front of her, rifle in my hands, tears in my eyes.

And they were certainly a marvelous thing, those tears, not only for
her, but for me as well.

My mother . . .

My mother was lying on her back,
her eyes were closed, and she seemed to be asleep;
Even her hand, abandoned on the sheets,
had dozed off.

I fell silent,
looking at the moon rising inch by inch
over the olive trees of Settignano.
It gave me great solace,
that moon and those trees.
That bright silver moon over silvery trees,
that moon in the shape of an olive leaf,
clean and transparent,
shining like a vein of silver, pulsing
through green marble
in the incensed darkness of a church.

Six Winds

(1956)

You can recognize a place by the way it breathes,
by the breath of the land itself;
by the breeze that combs the needles of the pines
and turns the olive leaves a lighter green;
by the wind that ruffles the hair of young girls,
smoothes the stone walls,
and polishes the skies of those unsettled days in March.

Here, too, we have our own way of breathing,
different from our neighbors
(but to say *different* is not enough:
better to say *opposite*).
Our stones, rivers, forests, lakes and people
all rise and fall together with the same breath.

Like our neighbors, though,
we are visited by the Four Winds,
which come from somewhere else and pass on by.
They do not stay long enough to shape our character
or give texture to our skin and earth,
or color to our eyes and leaves.

From the east the *Grecale* carries the strong perfume
of horses and sheep:
warm air veined with the smoke
of ancient fires outside Etruscan tombs,
rich with the fragrances
of fresh cheese set out to dry on beds of aromatic herbs,
of cauldrons full of boiling ricotta,
of sheepskins nailed to the doors of cabins,
of cracked mud drying in the sun
ready to dissolve with the first rains of autumn.
In it you can detect the musk of wild boar,
the blood of slaughtered hogs,
the sweat of black buffalo
pushing with their broad chests through wild reeds and rushes.
In it you can smell the ancient ferment
of thick yellow tomb-stone pumice
mixed with the fresh blue scent of alabaster,
the chalky limestone of ancient columns,
the dusty brick of aqueducts,
and the smooth green marble of the church.

A good wind, the *Grecale*. But not homemade.

The western *Libeccio* hits suddenly—crazy and violent—
a thief on the run from a Spanish prison,
making up for lost time.
It drives the waves against the whitened shore
like a herd of maddened sheep,
plummets like a falcon onto folded sails,
sending shredded strips of canvas flapping like frightened doves
into the whirlwind.
Its long and angry whistle, sharp as a blade,
scythes the grassy pastures
scattering herds of grazing horses in a foamy-maned gallop

across a green sea streaked with long white neighings.
Thousands of half-naked prisoners break loose
from the dungeons of Spain
bellowing for joy,
joined by drunken sailors clambering
down the sides of ships wrecked in the storm,
their tongues cracked and swollen with scurvy.
Dogs howl from the mountaintops
whipping the waves into a frenzy.
Clouds of dust swirl through the streets,
and a metallic fog infiltrates the cities,
overruns the countryside,
sowing the bitter taste of salt in the mouths
of prisoners on their mats, invalids in their beds,
monks in their cells, lunatics in their asylums,
peasants in the countryside, foresters on the mountain.
Everywhere there is running, shrieking:
Libeccio! Libeccio!
Shouting boys escape from school,
the shore churns white with foam.

A beautiful wind, the *Libeccio.* But not homemade.

The southern *Scirocco* strolls up from Elba, soft and sweaty:
a lazy, loafing wind, loitering around street-corners
leaving behind the stink of tobacco and wine,
of rotten fish and tar.
A fat potbellied wind, with wrinkled skin
and wide hairy hands that wipe across your mouth,
caress your cheeks, slide along your arms
and down the crest of your spine,
tracing a soft crease of sweat wherever it has been.
Enormous spiders drift crookedly through the air
on invisible threads.

Dead lizards lie upside down along the walls,
flaunting their swollen white bellies.
The sky is grey and heavy:
anything copper turns a moldy green,
dirty clouds fringed in yellow rub up against the walls,
and greasy waves give birth to worn-out shoes and dead fish.

An ugly wind, the *Scirocco*. But not homemade.

The northern *Tramontano* descends in a torrent,
carrying along with it, like a river in flood,
the surging odor of chestnut and broom,
of warm stables, oak forests, the smoke
of twig fires in fireplaces of white stone.
If it is sometimes called *Arrotino*—knife-grinder—
that is because it whittles the cypresses
into slender green daggers aimed at heaven.
The air, purified, resonates like a sheet of glass,
and the sky bends and recedes,
outlining the mountains sharp against its pale smooth blue.
The roads seem whiter than usual,
the river sparkles against its banks,
a calm settles into the houses
filling glasses, bottles and bowls
with a blue serenity.

A beautiful wind, the *Tramontano*. But not homemade.

Then there is a young adolescent wind,
an orphan, from nowhere in particular.
Most call it the *Passerotto,*
since it hops like a sparrow through hedges and fields,
caressing the faces of housewives with its wings.
It brushes the coats of cattle and horses,

polishes the windowpanes,
and transforms the grapes into lively shining eyes
that peek at you from behind the vines.
A little orphan wind that blesses the olives,
but no one knows from where it comes.
Some say Umbria,
others Marche or even further.
It is clean, clear and civil,
a wind which makes things simpler, leaner.
It is favored by the people of Siena,
and you will see it in their paintings,
just as you can feel it blowing through the sermons of San
    Bernardino,
and hear it flowing like water
down the marble facades of their churches
and the walls of their convents.

A gay wind, the *Passerotto.* But not homemade.

Then there is the Wind With No Name,
homemade,
Tuscan from head to heel.
It sucks the *T*'s and *C*'s from our mouths.
It softens certain *T*'s into *Th*'s,
changes the *Ci* into *Gi* in Versilia,
hardens the *S* into *Z* in Pistoia.
It is a wind made to measure by our hands,
kneaded in our kitchens like dough,
then gnawed by our teeth and tongues.

You can see it blowing through the foliage of Giotto's trees,
moving behind the eyes
and across the foreheads of Masaccio's youths,
in the landscapes of Francesca, Leonardo, and Lippi,

in the verses of Cavalcanti and Guinizelli,
in the prose of Dino Compagni and Machiavelli.
It is the wind of Pulci, Berni, Cellini,
Dante and Boccaccio.

Wherever it chooses, it leaves its mark,
though it could just as easily pick your pocket
without letting you know.
If it sometimes adorns itself,
it does so reluctantly,
since it uses adornments rarely,
and more out of spite than courtesy,
never conforming to the rounded mouths
of those who would become Tuscan
by becoming refined.

To breathe it properly, you need to be born here.
Otherwise, it can make you cough,
or give you a bellyache, or even worse:
distend your throat
(a horrible thing to see,
at least as far as we are concerned).

It has a slightly bitter aftertaste,
like our olive oil,
like real Chianti,
like the fish plucked from the Arno,
like the wit, the smile, the irony,
the suave urbanity of real Tuscans,
who are witty-smiling-ironic
and courteous in fashion and words, but
in the end, how bitter!

What a sad, severe sense of history,
what an astute, wicked, abandoned sense of human misery,
in souls who on the surface seem so smooth and nonchalant.
That famous common sense of the Tuscans:
what a convenient alibi!
And what a deceptively serene prospect we offer—
so lithe, thin, sly—to those who do not know us
(or pretend not to know us out of prudence or laziness).
You would do well to guard against our suave urbanity,
our nonchalant smoothness.

If the Wind With No Name blows along the ground,
woe if you misstep:
you have been walking on a razor's edge.
If it blows from above, it does so on purpose
to make you look up,
and then woe if you stumble:
suddenly the sky, the clouds, the roofs,
the walls, the towers, the belfries,
all Tuscans and all of Tuscany will descend upon you,
to crush and trample you.
And not content with having murdered you,
will leave you for a fool.

It is wise not to joke with such a wind,
since no one knows its paternity.
There are those who say that, like all things Tuscan,
it comes from below.

Or more precisely, as the Etruscans believed,
that it comes from Hell.

Two Sisters

(1936)

Written when Malaparte was in exile on the isle of Lipari

Clara and Suni sat at the garden's edge,
where the carpet of pine needles unraveled
revealing a floor of wet and shining sand.
The juniper and tamarisk rustled softly,
and the sea swelled at their feet
with the calm, deep breath of a sleeping horse.

Above the darkening garden the first stars were being born,
slowly bleeding one by one into the purity of the air.
Shells scattered along the beach
lit up with starry reflections,
cobwebs glinted in the grass,
and the two sisters sat, holding hands,
and let the silent river of the night
carry them off toward an obscure horizon.

Ever since she became aware that she was still a child,
Suni could never lift her gaze to the sky
without feeling lost and insignificant.

There is Orion, she said, softly.
Orion was a present she gave herself,
a sweet and mortal present.

Orion returning home from the hunt,
with his bow slung across his shoulders,
following his Dog, who carefully flushed the bushes for game,
startling the Dove, who flew off in terror,
frightening the Hare, who sprang suddenly
from under a cover of white cloud,
disappearing between golden sheaves of grain.

Then Altair, Izar, Shedir, Alderamin,
Algorab, Betelgeuse, Bellatrix, and Alcor:
stars with magic names
gradually taking on the human aspect they assumed
in the chart with the great baroque frame
at the entrance to the old house:

Andromeda chained to the rock,
hair loosened over naked shoulders,
her white arms reaching out toward Perseus,
magnificent and sad,
holding the serpent-haired head of Medusa
in his upraised fist.
Aurix in his chariot,
snapping the reins above his horses' flaming crests
as they streaked through the tumult in a cloud of red dust
lit by the green lightning of clashing swords and shields.

The Bull, carrying Europa on his foamy black back,
and further on, beyond the Bear,
Pegasus, winged and prancing,

and Cassiopeia, and the Pleiades, and the Swan, and the Fox
and closer, the Dioscures, high in the sky
on horseback, as in Euripides's *Hélène,*
surrounded by the Lizard and the Fish,
swimming in deep blue water.
And the Serpent, drowsy and treacherous in the grass.

It was a baroque sky,
inhabited by sumptuous characters,
like the stage of a theater.
Clara would have preferred a sky more like the sea,
an immense and deserted sea
where the stars would swim like schools of fish,
or float like dead leaves, algae, or jellyfish,
herded by the wind toward a rosy dawn.

But Suni preferred to imagine it like this,
crowded with living people, monsters and animals,
and Orion, her beloved Orion,
near the horizon, with his bow over his shoulder,
wearing beautiful silver-buckled sandals,
following his Dog with the lustrous coat of green fur.

She looked at her sky
and remembered all the clear autumn nights
spent in wonder at the dazzling and distant constellations
hanging above the depths of the garden,
with Orion disappearing into a purple mist,
and a sweet sadness came over her.
A sadness already disturbed and uncertain.

She felt Clara's hand breathing lightly in her own,
and in the dim light

she was just able to distinguish Clara's cheek
submerged in a golden wave of loosened hair
tossed gently back and forth by the wind.
Maybe Clara was sad, too.

Suni had a vague intuition that in her sister's heart
a cauldron of thoughts and feelings unknown to her
was starting to simmer,
and she was jealous of Clara's serene acceptance
of the sweet, useless mysteries of adolescence.

Now Clara is going to turn, thought Suni,
And when she looks at me I will see in her eyes
a secret fear, an unexpected dread.

They had grown up together:
Suni was thirteen, a little younger than Clara.
but even when she was tiny,
still wrapped in the sadnesses of childhood,
she felt distant from these new uncertainties,
already a stranger to the open curiosity of adolescence.

Clara was fifteen:
there was something deeply changed about her smile,
about her gaze, her voice.
A kind of intuition, or perhaps regret,
an indefinite hope.
She was sad, too, looking up,
ready to fly away into the sky,
into that unknown world,
among those heroes, those prancing horses,
those monsters with the eyes of newborn babes.

Suni did not dare look at her sister,
imagining that at any moment they would have to say goodbye.
They had shared until today the dreams, the illusions,
the hopes of childhood,
but now Clara was going to embark without her
on that mysterious voyage into adolescence,
a voyage from which she might not ever return.

And then Suni would sit at the edge of the sea,
alone, at the edge of the sky,
in this garden, alone,
in this house where they had lived together for so long,
twinned by the same desires and fears.

Do you know, said Clara,
I seem to be far from here. So far away.

Far from me, too? said Suni,
staring hopelessly at her silver Orion.

From you, too.
Far from everything. I want you to come with me,
to never leave me.

I will come with you, said Suni.

But she had never felt so sad and abandoned.
She looked sideways at the sweet curve of Clara's shoulders,
the shadowy pink hollow of her pulsing throat,
the fruit of her lips nectared with scarlet blood.

Clara was already undoing the warm and comfortable
lacing of childhood dreams:

she was a dancer in the wings,
eyes brimming with lively shadows,
bending her knee, stretching her arms,
trying out the first steps of the dance.

I'm afraid, she whispered,
and a gentle shiver slid across her shoulders.

Suni grasped Clara's arm and squeezed it hard.
She felt part of a shy and innocent secret.

Do you know, said Clara,
Last night I dreamed that Mom took me by the hand,
separated me gently from you,
and she and I went together like two sisters
down a long road.
Mom leaned close to look at me,
and it seemed that she had your eyes,
your forehead, your mouth:
she was going to be my sister from now on,
a new sister.
I woke up in tears
to think that I had left you here, waiting for me.

Suni let go of Clara's arm,
a lump in her throat.
Yes, that is the way it was:
a dark cloud gathered in her heart,
a jealous resignation.

Suni imagined Clara and her mother
holding hands like the Two Sisters
as they walked across the warm and transparent sky.

Clara would not look back,
full of sad and stubborn regret.
But her mother turned from time to time
and Suni saw her smile shimmering
from the deep immensity of the sky,
like a mirage of water from beyond the horizon.

She closed her eyes,
rested her head on Clara's shoulder
and watched as the Two Sisters
took their place in the starry sky,
welcomed by Andromeda
who reached out to them with her naked arms
as the Swan, the Lizard, the Fish,
the Bull, the Serpent gathered around;
and Orion, with his Dog,
and the Hare, leaping.

Are you asleep? asked Clara,
leaning over her sister.

No, Suni was not asleep.
It was a kind of dizziness:
an immense wave had suddenly fallen from the sky
and swallowed her up.
She couldn't speak.
her mouth was full of a bitter blue light.

I am happy, sighed Clara,
pulling her sister closer.

Me too, whispered Suni.
Me too. Oh yes, me too.

She began to cry silently,
face buried in Clara's shoulder.
She felt unbearably sad, abandoned, insignificant,
betrayed.

But the betrayal lay sweetly in her heart,
the last betrayal of childhood,
the first revelation of adolescence.

Today We Fly

(1936)

During his teens, Malaparte was a student at the Collegio
Cicognini in Prato, about sixteen kilometers from Florence.
The event described in this story—the flight of Romolo
Manissero from Florence to Prato in a Blériot biplane—
occurred on May 11, 1911.

One Sunday morning,
instead of studying *The Iliad*,
I escaped with Bino to Florence,
to see what miracles the aviator Manissero
would perform.

Whether he would demonstrate the art of Daedalus
or the folly of Icarus.

We found the whole city festooned with banners
on which was written: *Today We Fly*.
They were everywhere: Via Cerretani,
Via Cavour, Via Calzaioli, along the embankments.
There was even one stretched across the Arno
with an enormous red *Today We Fly*

reflected in the yellow water
like the famous *In Hoc Signo Vinces* of Ponte Milvio.

We almost expected that Florence itself
would lift off,
with its towers, its statues, its red roofs,
with its cathedral's nodding cupola
rising slowly through the clouds
like a balloon.

Every window, doorway and marketplace
was crammed with upturned faces,
scanning the sky for some sign
of the direction the wind might take,
and whether there would come with it
the smell of rain.

We were most afraid of the wind from Bologna,
proud enemy to the north.
Almost as bad would have been the wind from the south,
from Empoli, called the *scirocco;*
or Petrarch's east wind from Arezzo,
with its Grecian-accented gusts.
But even a soft westerly breeze from Pistoia—
even that sweet breath from the ballads of Cino,
full of *dolce stil novo*—
would have spelled disaster.

Luckily the sky that Sunday was clear,
and the air was still.
The leaves on the trees around the parade ground
stood at ease,
and the outlines of the hills were crisp,
sharply etched in the crystalline air.

Just wait. Today we really will fly,
said Bino with a smile.

For overnight *Today We Fly* had become a catchphrase,
fit for every occasion:
for a straw hat rolling along the pavement;
for a parasol blown around the corner;
for a dress tangled up between the knees,
or blown flapping like a flag around rounded hips.

It was the happy time of the first aeroplanes,
before the War
when it was fashionable for women
to wear enormous hairdos
as wide as their dresses were narrow.
And those gigantic wings of hair,
which were the objects of so many of our teenage jokes,
have remained braided together in my heart
with the fluttering *Today We Fly:*
maliciously good-natured mementos
of my adolescence.

We hurried over to the parade grounds,
and there was Manissero
crouched in the cockpit of his machine:
a contraption of woven reeds and papery cloth,
with a motor so small it made you think a horsefly
was pinned to the frame behind his shoulders.

The crowd had assembled, holding its breath,
waiting for the miracle to happen,
when suddenly the leaves began to tremble,
and the blades of grass to nod.
A few tiny white clouds sprouted

like windowsills on Monte Morello,
and the women's wings of hair began to come untucked
from their padded nests of false braids.

Manissero jumped out of his cockpit
at the first sign of this unfortunate breeze,
waved amicably to the crowd with a gloved hand,
and yanked off his leather helmet
while a banner was unfurled above the grandstands:

Because of Unsettled Weather, Today We Will Not Fly.

It was hard to imagine anything more settled
than the weather that day:
a magnificent, paradisiacal Sunday in spring.
But all it took was this delicate breeze,
this perfumed zephyr from Pistoia,
to spoil everything.

We returned to Prato with heavy hearts,
and I took up my study of the abandoned *Iliad*,
quiet and discouraged.

Thursday morning the rumor began to spread
that the following Sunday,
if the weather was favorable,
Manissero would attempt to fly
from Florence to Prato and back:
thirty kilometers round trip!

By Saturday, Via Magnolfi, the Corso,
Via del'Oche, Via Firenzuola—all the streets of Prato
were crisscrossed with white banners
carrying those fateful words:

Today We Fly.

By noon Sunday
rivers of people from the surrounding countryside
were flooding into the city through its five gates.
and by three o'clock
the cathedral square was awash
with a restless and noisy crowd,
pale, perspiring, noses in the air.
I stood among them with my classmates,
all of us impatient, barely kept in check
by the stern gaze of our principal
and the softer reprimands of the teachers.

We began to hear a new word:
Velivolo!
dancing above the buzz of the crowd.
But that name for aeroplane, recently coined by d'Annunzio,
seemed too delicate for the gaping mouths of dumbstruck farmers:
it was still fresh, still smelled of varnish,
and was as sweet and sharp in the mouth
as mint candy.
Velivolo!

Suddenly a white wing appeared in the blue sky
and the reed–and–paper bird
grew larger, came closer,
hovered over the cathedral square.

A cry, only one, but from a thousand throats;
a cry more of fear than joy:
then sudden silence,
bursting with anguish.
Manissero was perhaps two hundred meters above our heads,

and it seemed miraculous.
Miraculous not just because he was flying,
but because he was flying over Prato,
in the virgin sky of Prato!
which only the kites of children had dared to caress
until today.

As long as the flying was over Florence,
things were fine:
certain facts, in Florence, are understandable,
are legitimate, and fit within the logic of history.

But over Prato!
Over Prato where for centuries now
nothing miraculous had happened.
Not on the ground,
and not in the sky.
Especially not in the sky.

Over Prato!
Where it seemed that miracles had become impossible,
caught as we were
between the historic pride of Florence
and the ancient jealousy of Pistoia.
Sacrificed,
reduced to poor relations,
robbed not only of everything that we had,
which would have been bad enough,
but of everything we might have wanted to have.

Yet here was Manissero flying in our sky,
in the neglected sky of Prato.
And he was flying, or so it seemed,

better than he might have flown in the sky of Florence.
Better than in any other sky in Tuscany!

After a moment, though, the suspicion began to grow
that he might fly as far as Pistoia.
Everyone held their breath,
balanced on one foot,
hearts stopped between beats:

The treacherous sky of Pistoia!

Some of us took out our keys,
ready to rattle them against such a betrayal.
The rest of us set our lips
to whistle in defiance.
But Manissero veered to the right,
and after a wide turn over Prato
he headed back toward Florence.

The city detonated with joy.
I lost myself in the crowd, beyond thought,
proud citizen of Prato to my bones.
It wouldn't be too much to say that all of us, that day,
felt we held a piece of sky in our hands.

That night, in my dreams, the Achaean army,
assembling beneath the walls of Troy,
came to a halt, astonished at what lay before them:
stretching from tower to tower
immense white banners
on which great red letters spelled out:
Today We Fly.

And then Troy, the city of Priam—
which from a distance resembled nothing more than Prato—
detached itself gently from the earth,
hovered with its banners snapping in the breeze,
and drifted away into the clear sky,
swinging gently from side to side.

Maddened Achilles ran along below, commanding:
Stop! Stop!

And from the buzz of his accent
you might have thought he was from Pistoia.

Beloved Priam, from the top of the Trojan gates,
answered sweetly:
Too Late. Too Late.

And his voice had all the soft accents of Prato,
taking flight.

El Traidor

(1966)

From Malaparte's journal when he was living in Paris, 1948

In February 1942 during the siege of Leningrad I found myself attached
to General Edqvist, the commander of a division of Finnish troops
stationed near Lake Ladoga. One morning he asked me to pay him a
visit.

We have just taken eighteen Spanish prisoners, he said.

Spanish? I said. *Now you're at war with Spain?*

I don't know anything about that, he said. *But I have eighteen prisoners
who speak Spanish and claim they are Spanish, not Russian.*

Very strange.

We have to interrogate them. Of course, you speak Spanish.

No, actually I don't.

*Well, you're Italian, so you're more Spanish than I am. Go interrogate
them.*

I did as I was told. I found the prisoners under guard in barracks. I
asked whether they were Russian or Spanish. I spoke in Italian, slowly,
and they answered in Spanish, slowly, and we understood each other
perfectly.

We are soldiers in the Soviet army, but we are Spanish.

One of them went on to say that they were orphans of the Spanish

Civil War; their parents had been killed in the bombardments and reprisals. One day they were all put on board a Soviet ship in Barcelona and sent to Russia, where they were fed and clothed, where they learned a trade, and where they eventually became soldiers in the Red Army.

But we are Spanish.

In fact, I remembered reading at the time that the Russians had evacuated thousands of Red Republican children to the USSR to save them from the bombardments and famine of the Spanish Civil War.

Are you members of the Communist Party? I asked.

Naturally.

Well, keep quiet about it. You've told me, and for the moment that's enough. Don't tell anyone else. Do you understand?

No, we don't understand.

That doesn't matter. If I stop to think about it, I don't understand it either. It's just that I think it would be better if you didn't tell anyone else you are members of the Communist Party.

No, we can't accept such a compromise. We were taught to tell the truth. There is nothing wrong about being Communist. We won't hide the fact that we are Communists.

All right, do as you wish. Meanwhile, you should know that the Finnish people are honest and humane, that among the men in the Finnish army there are many Communists but they are fighting against the Russians who invaded their country in 1939. So being Communist or not has no fundamental importance, that's what I want to say. But you understand me, I think.

No, we don't. We understand you are spouting propaganda, that's all.

No, that's not all. You should know that I will do everything possible to make sure you are not harmed. Do you understand?

Yes.

All right then. Goodbye. I will come and see you tomorrow.

I found General Edqvist and told him about my conversation.

What can we do? the general asked me. *You know, their situation is extremely precarious. They are Communists, Spanish volunteers in the Red Army. Of course they were children when they were evacuated, so they aren't responsible for the education they were given. If it were up to me, I would help them. But under the circumstances, the best thing would be for you to telegraph your friend de Foxá, the Spanish ambassador in Helsinki. Ask him to come at my request. I will turn the prisoners over to him and he can do what he wants with them.*

I sent a cable to de Foxá: *Have eighteen Spanish prisoners come quickly take them in consignment.*

Two days later, during a blizzard, de Foxá arrived in a sleigh, the temperature forty-two degrees below zero. He was half-dead with cold and lack of sleep. As soon as he saw me he shouted:

What do you think you're doing? Why did you telegraph me? What can I do with eighteen Spanish Red Army soldiers? Put them up at the embassy? Now I have to sort things out. You are a meddler.

And you are the Spanish ambassador.

Yes, but of Franco's Spain. And these kids are Communists. At any rate, I'll do what I can. But I would really like to know why you got mixed up with this.

He was furious. But de Foxá had a good heart, and I knew that he would do everything possible to help. He went to see the prisoners, and I tagged along.

I am the ambassador of Franco's Spain, de Foxá said to them. *I am Spanish, you are Spanish, I came to help. What can I do for you?*

For us? Nothing, said the prisoners. *We don't want to have anything to do with a representative of Franco's Spain.*

Do you think this is some kind of a joke? It took me two days and two nights to get here and now you're sending me away? Nevertheless, I'll do everything in my power to help you. Francisco Franco knows how to forgive.

Franco is our enemy. He killed our parents. We're just asking you to leave us alone.

De Foxá went to find General Edqvist.

They're stubborn, he said. *But I will do my duty anyway. I'll telegraph the ministry in Madrid for instructions, and then we'll do whatever Madrid says.*

The next day, de Foxá prepared to leave for Helsinki.

Mind your own business, you understand? he said, getting into his sleigh. *It's your fault that I'm in this jam, you hear me?*

Adiós, Agustin.

Adiós, Malaparte.

A few days later, one of the prisoners fell ill. The doctor said: *Inflammation of the lungs. Very dangerous.*

We have to let de Foxá know, said General Edqvist.

So I telegraphed de Foxá: *One prisoner sick, very serious, come quickly with medicine chocolate cigarettes.*

Two days later, de Foxá arrived in his sleigh. He was furious.

Now what have you done? he shouted as soon as he saw me. *Is it my fault that this kid got sick? What can I do? I am alone in Helsinki, you know, without an attaché—no assistants, nothing, I have to do everything myself. And you make me snowshoe around Finland in a blizzard, all because of your meddling.*

Listen, he's sick, he's dying, it's good that you're here. You represent Spain.

All right, all right, let's go and see him.

De Foxá had brought a huge amount of medicine, food, cigarettes, warm clothes. He really did things royally, my old pal Agustin.

The sick soldier recognized de Foxá, and even smiled. His comrades, though, stood back silent and hostile, staring at Agustin with disdain and hatred.

De Foxá stayed for two days, then he went back to Helsinki. Before getting in his sleigh, he said:

Malaparte, why do you keep getting mixed up with things that don't concern you? When will you learn to just leave me in peace? You aren't Spanish, you know. Leave me alone.

Adiós, Agustin.

Adiós, Malaparte.

Three days later, the soldier died of his inflammation. General Edqvist summoned me:

I could have him buried in the Finnish custom. But I think it would be better to let de Foxá know. After all, this soldier was Spanish. What do you think?

Yes, we should tell de Foxá. It would be the diplomatic thing to do.

And so I sent a telegram: *Soldier just died come quick need to bury.*

Two days later, de Foxá arrived. He was furious.

Will you stop harassing me? he shouted as soon as he saw me. *This is driving me crazy! Of course once you let me know that this kid is dead and has to be buried, it's impossible for me not to come. But what if you just hadn't told me? It's not as if my coming here is going to revive him.*

No, but you are Spain. We can't just bury him like a dog, in these woods, far from his country, from Spain. At least, with you here, everything is different, you know? It's as if all of Spain is here.

Naturally, said de Foxá. *That's why I came. But why do you get mixed up in these things? You are not Spanish, válgame Dios!*

He has to be buried properly, Agustin. That's why I contacted you.

Yes, I know, I know. Let's move on. Where is he?

We went to see the poor kid, who was laid out in the barracks surrounded by his comrades. They stared at de Foxá with a somber, almost menacing defiance.

We will bury him, said de Foxá, *according to Catholic ritual. Spaniards are Catholic. I want him to be buried like a true Spaniard, a good Spanish soldier.*

We will not allow that, said one of the prisoners. *Our comrade was an atheist, as are all of us. This must be honored. We will not permit him to be buried as a Catholic.*

I represent Spain, and the deceased was Spanish, a Spanish citizen. I will have him buried as a Catholic. Do you understand?

No, we don't.

I am the ambassador of Spain, and I will do my duty! If you don't understand me, I don't care.

And with that, de Foxá turned and went outside.

Agustin, my friend, I said, *General Edqvist is a gentleman. He wouldn't like it if you forced your opinions on a dead man. Finnish people are freethinkers, they will not understand your position. We have to find some compromise.*

Yes, but I am Franco's ambassador! I cannot bury a Spaniard without Catholic ritual. Mi Dios! Why didn't you just go ahead and bury him without me? You see what you've done, with your obsession for getting mixed up in things that don't concern you?

All right, don't worry, it will all turn out for the best.

We went to see the general.

Evidently, said the general, *if the deceased was a Communist, an atheist, as his comrades say and as I believe he was, it won't be possible to bury him as a Catholic. I am aware, however, that the ambassador represents Spain, and can't officiate at a burial without Catholic rites. What shall we do, I wonder?*

I suggested that we send for the only Catholic priest in Helsinki, an Italian. (There was also a Catholic bishop in Helsinki, from the Netherlands, but it was unthinkable to ask a bishop to come the front.) So we telegraphed the priest, and two days later he arrived. He was from upper Lombardy—a highlander, very simple, direct, and pure. He grasped the situation immediately and set about arranging things for the best.

The burial took place the next day. In a clearing in the woods where the little cemetery was located, a grave had been blasted by dynamite out of the frozen earth. A group of Finnish soldiers was arranged along one side of the grave, and the flag of Franco's Spain had been placed at the bottom. The snow covering the ground nearby glowed softly in the milky daylight. The coffin was carried by four of the prisoners, followed in procession by Ambassador de Foxá, General Edqvist, myself, the Spanish prisoners, and finally by a few Finnish soldiers. The priest kept himself apart, about fifty feet away. His lips moved, reciting the prayers for the dead—but in silence, out of respect for the opinions of the deceased. When the coffin was lowered into the grave, the Finnish soldiers, all Protestants, discharged their rifles. General Edqvist and the Finnish officers and soldiers all saluted with elbows bent, as did I; Ambassador de Foxá saluted with his arm straight out, palm flat, in the Fascist manner; and the comrades of the deceased also held their arms straight out, but with fists closed.

The next day de Foxá prepared to leave. Before settling into his sleigh for the ride back, he took me aside and confided:

I want to thank you for all you've done. You've been very thoughtful and considerate. Excuse me if I was angry, but you know . . . You are always getting mixed up in things that don't concern you!

A few days passed. The prisoners waited for the response from Madrid, which did not come. General Edqvist grew increasingly nervous.

You know, he said, *I can't keep these men here much longer. A decision has to be made: either Spain takes them, or I send them to a concentration camp. Their situation is delicate. It is better to hold them here, but I can't keep them forever.*

Have a little patience. We will get a response.

The response arrived: *Only those prisoners who declare themselves to be Spanish, who recognize the government of Francisco Franco, and who express the desire to return to Spain, will be recognized as Spanish citizens.*

Go and explain the situation to them, said General Edqvist.

We do not recognize the government of Franco, the prisoners said, *and we do not want to return to Spain.*

I respect the firmness of your opinions, I said, *but you should appreciate how delicate your predicament is. If you admit to fighting as part of the Red Army, you will all be shot. The laws of war are the laws of war. So make it possible for me to help you. Consider this carefully. Basically, you are Spaniards. All the Republicans still in Spain have accepted the legitimacy of Franco. They lost the game, and their loyalty to their cause does not prevent them from realizing that Franco won. Do what the Republicans in Spain have done. Accept your defeat.*

There are no more Republicans in Spain. They have all been shot.

Where did you hear that story?

We read it in the Soviet newspapers. We will not recognize the Franco regime. We would rather be shot by the Finnish than by Franco.

Listen, I've had it with you, with Communist Spain, with Fascist Spain, with Russia! But I can't abandon you, I will not abandon you. I will do everything in my power to help. If you don't want to recognize the Franco regime, I will sign the declarations in your name. That will be perjury, but it will save your lives. Understand?

No. We will say that you forged our signatures. We just want you to leave us alone! Don't get involved in things that don't concern you. Are you Spanish? No. So why are you getting involved in this?

I am not Spanish, but I am a man, a Christian, and I will not abandon you. I repeat: let me help you. You will go back to Spain, and once you are there you will act like all the rest, like all the other Republicans who have accepted defeat. You are young, and I will not let you die.

Just leave us alone!

I went away, dispirited.

We have to tell de Foxá, General Edqvist said. *Telegraph him that he needs to come and settle this situation.*

I telegraphed de Foxá: *Prisoners refuse come quick persuade them.*

Two days later, de Foxá arrived. The north wind blew with unusual violence; de Foxá was covered with frost. As soon as he saw me, he shouted:

Again! Why telegraph me? What good did you think it would do? These kids won't listen to me. You don't know the Spanish. They are as stubborn as the mules of Toledo.

Go and talk to them, I said. *Perhaps . . .*

Yes, yes I know. That's why I came. But really, Malaparte . . .

He went to see the prisoners, and I accompanied him. They were resolute. De Foxá pleaded with them, cajoled them, threatened them. Nothing worked.

So we will be shot. And then? they said.

And then I will have you buried as Catholics! shouted de Foxá boiling with rage, tears in his eyes. Agustin was a good man, and he was suffering from this magnificent and terrible stubbornness.

You would not do that, said the prisoners. *Usted es un hombre honesto.* They were moved as well, in spite of themselves.

In turmoil, de Foxá prepared to leave. He urged General Edqvist to hold the prisoners a bit longer, and to do nothing without telling him. Once he was installed in his sleigh, he turned to me:

You see, Malaparte, it's your fault I am in such a state. I don't want to think of the fate of these poor kids. I admire them, I am proud of them—real Spaniards. Yes, they are real Spaniards, loyal and brave. You know . . . ?

There were tears in his eyes, and his voice trembled.

We have to do whatever we can to save them. I am counting on you, he said.

I will do my best. I promise I won't let them die. Adiós, Agustin.

Adiós, Malaparte.

I went every day to talk to the prisoners, trying to persuade them, but it was hopeless.

Thank you, they would say, *but we are Communists, and will never recognize Franco.*

A few days later, General Edqvist called for me.

Go and see what is happening with the prisoners. They have almost killed one of their comrades. We don't know why.

I went to see the prisoners. One of them was sitting by himself in a corner of the room, covered with blood, guarded by a Finnish soldier armed with a *Suomi-konepistooli,* the famous Finnish submachine gun.

What have you done to this man?

He's a traitor, they answered. *Un traidor.*

Is this true? I said to the wounded man.

Yes. I am a traitor. I want to return to Spain. I can't take it any more. I don't want to die. I want to go back to Spain. I am Spanish. I want to go back to Spain.

He is a traitor! Un traidor! said his comrades, looking at him with stares full of hate.

I had *el traidor* placed by himself in another barrack, and telegraphed de Foxá: *One soldier wants to return to Spain come quick.* Two days later, de Foxá arrived. He was blinded by the snow; his face had been pelted by chunks of ice which the hooves of the horses had chipped from the frozen road.

What are you doing? Why do you keep meddling in things that don't concern you? When will you stop harassing me with this nonsense? Where is this soldier?

Over there, Agustin.

All right, let's go see him.

El traidor welcomed us in silence. He was a boy of about twenty, blond, with blue eyes, very pale. He was blond the way Spaniards are blond, he had blue eyes the way Spaniards are blue-eyed. He began to cry. He said: *I am a traitor. Yo un traidor. But I can't take it any more. I don't want to die. I want to go back to Spain.* He cried, and his eyes were full of fear, hope, supplication.

De Foxá was moved.

Stop crying, he said. *We will send you back to Spain. You will be welcomed there. You will be pardoned. It wasn't your fault if the Russians made you into a Communist. You were just a kid. Don't cry.*

I am a traitor, said the prisoner.

We are all traitors, de Foxá said brusquely, quietly.

The next day, de Foxá had him sign the declaration and prepared to leave. Before doing so, he went to see General Edqvist.

You are a gentleman, he said. *Give me your word that you will help the rest of these poor kids. They would rather die rather than renounce their beliefs.*

Yes, they are good kids, said General Edqvist. *I am a soldier, and I admire courage and loyalty even in our enemies. I give you my word. Besides, I agree with Marshal Mannerheim: they will be treated as prisoners of war. Don't worry, I will answer for their lives.*

De Foxá shook General Edqvist's hand in silence, choked by emotion. When he was settled in his sleigh, he smiled, finally:

At last, he said, *you are done annoying me. I'll telegraph Madrid, and as soon as I have an answer, we'll know where things stand. Thank you, Malaparte.*

Adiós, Agustin.

Adiós.

A few days later, the answer came from Madrid. The prisoner was taken to Helsinki, where Spanish officers were waiting for him. *El traidor* was flown to Berlin, and on from there to Spain. It was clear that the Spanish authorities wanted to make something out of this. The prisoner was overwhelmed with care and attention, and he took it all joyfully.

Two months later, I returned to Helsinki. It was spring. The trees were covered with a foam of tender green leaves, birds singing in their branches. I went to fetch de Foxá from his villa at Brunnsparken, and we strolled along the Esplanade, heading towards Kämp. The sea was so green it seemed also to be bursting with leaves, and the little island of Suomenlinna was white with the wings of seagulls.

And the prisoner, el traidor? Any news?

Again? shouted de Foxá. *Why do you keep meddling in this business?*

I did something to help save his life, I said.

De Foxá told me that *el traidor* had been warmly welcomed in Madrid. He was paraded around, and the people said: *See this handsome boy? He was a Communist, he fought with the Russians, he was taken prisoner on the Russian front. But he wanted to come home, to Spain. He has recognized Franco. He is a brave boy, a good Spaniard.*

He was taken to the cafés, the theaters, bullrings, stadiums, cinemas.

But he said: *You think this is a café? You should see the cafés in Moscow.*

And he laughed:

This is a theater? A cinema? You should see what they have in Moscow!

And he laughed. They took him to the stadium. He shouted out:

This is a stadium? You should see the stadium in Kiev.

And he laughed. Everyone turned to look at him, and he shouted: *You think this is a stadium? The stadium in Kiev, now that's a stadium!*

And he laughed.

Do you understand now? said de Foxá. *Do you finally understand? It's your fault they were furious with me at the ministry. It's all your fault. That should teach you to meddle in things that don't concern you!*

But el traidor—what did they do with him?

What did you want them to do with him? Nothing! They didn't do anything with him, said Agustin with a strange voice. *Why are you always getting involved?*

Then he smiled: *Anyway, they buried him as a Catholic.*

The Visit
of the Angel

(1936)

Written when Malaparte was in exile on the isle of Lipari, 1933–1934

Lavinia was on her way downstairs,
bare feet whispering on smooth stone steps,
when suddenly she paused,

interrupting the gentle cadence of her descent.
The unexpected silence woke me.
I waited, catching my breath.

The moon was gently rising
from her green hammock on the eastern horizon,
and though she had not yet disengaged
from the mountain's embrace,
already the sea resonated with her dense brilliance.

I called out: *Lavinia!*

The night remained silent, frozen,
an enormous beast crouching implacably
over forest and sea.

The island of Gorgona wandered like a distant sailboat
on the misty green horizon;
and the skiffs of fishermen floated serenely
from the mouth of the Magra,
their sails lighting up one by one
as they were touched by the moonlight.
Overturned hulls, on the deserted shore,
bulged from the sand with a rosy phosphorescence.

I called again: *Lavinia!*

Into the corridor, I leaned over the railing:
she was almost at the bottom of the stairs,
braced against the wall, motionless,
arms crossed over her breasts
in a gesture of ecstatic dismay.

She gestured for me to be quiet,
looking up with a blank stare
in which, for the first time,
the usual tenderness was veiled with hostility,
a radiance that was at the same time cruel and precise.
I crept downstairs and took her in my arms,
felt her collapse against me with the last of her strength.

The whole house was immersed in a thick and empty silence:
the shadows of trees flickered against the walls.
Outside, I could imagine the sand hissing
under the rhythmic caress of the waves.
And from time to time a gust would riffle through the pines,
drawing a murmured response from the oaks.

Lavinia half-smiled, ardent and astonished.
Her stare, now clearly focused,
lay deep at the back of her eyes.

And her hands, crossed over her breasts,
splashed a delicate and vibrant white
against the black of her robe.

Lavinia's pale features clouded over, and she trembled.
Suddenly I saw a transparent shadow
moving across the room.
Little by little, as my eyes adjusted to the darkness,
I saw that it was a barefoot child,
moving slowly, softly,
pausing from time to time
to listen to the murmuring of the trees
and the voice of the sea.

He did not seem to be aware of us,
or if he was it did not seem to matter,
but I would have sworn that this was not the first time
he had visited our house.
Nor could I help noticing
that as he walked he lifted his feet like a wounded bird,
sleepwalking with thoughtful grace.

Looking more closely, I saw that he had wings:
two little transparent wings tinged an indefinite blue
and spotted with silver, trembling like poplar leaves
on summer mornings.

Without question, this child was an Angel.
And if I had been waiting for him in vain,
if for many years I had been certain that the visit of an Angel
would signal the happiest moment of my life,
now that I finally saw him,
I was astonished by the anguished premonition
of some imminent disaster.

I wanted to speak to him,
to ask him to do us no harm,
nor to be cruel toward our poor happiness,
our insignificant and deluded happiness,
our proud hopes.
But caution held me back,
some intuition of which I felt as guilty
as of some secret and mortified desire.

From his way of walking, I had the impression
that he was dreaming of distant and unattainable pleasures,
and that he hid in his heart his own sad secret.
I thought perhaps he had come to share his sorrow with us,
to confess some angelic sin,
but his courage must have now failed him
and so he could not reveal the grief
which was so clearly consuming him.

And then he lifted his eyes to us.

Lavinia shrank back against me:
he looked beyond without seeing us
and moved some distance away,
stroking the furniture with his translucent, luminous hands,
caressing the books on the table,
the darkened lamps, the windowpanes.
Lavinia followed his movements
with a gaze that burned from her waxen face
like a fragile, intense flame.

Just at that moment, the moon untangled herself
from the sleepy embrace of the blue-shouldered mountains
and soared white and silent above the sea,
pouring the warmth of her immaculate light
into the glacial stillness of the air.

The Angel paused, transfixed, in front of the window,
his forehead against the glass.
Lavinia held her breath,
afraid that he might fly away into the sweetness of that light,
but he went over, slowly, to the far end of the room
and lay down with his hands under his cheek
in that universal gesture of sleep,
his wings breathing with a slow and even rhythm.

I had the impression that Lavinia
was overwhelmed by the desire, as well as the fear,
to see him up close,
perhaps to recognize him.
But the sleeping Angel was so dazzlingly lit
by the light from his silvery hair,
luminous hands and wings,
that it was impossible to see his face.

Certainly, Lavinia longed to believe
that he was the shining image of one of her joys,
one of her hopes, one of her sorrows.

But not only that:
there was a kind of familial complicity,
a maternal anxiety, an uncertain tenderness,
which every woman feels when confronted by an Angel.
As well as the expectation of some unforeseen event
which might explain the mystery of this apparition.

Or perhaps, like every woman confronted by an Angel,
Lavinia felt that her real femininity began from this moment,
that the Angel had come to reveal the secret
of a terrible and wondrous maternity,
a secret which kindles in every woman

a feeling for the divinity of her own entrails,
which makes of every woman the daughter of her own child.

At that moment, the Angel awoke,
raised himself up on one elbow,
and turned his face in our direction,
his eyelashes shining with a tender brilliance.
He seemed to become aware of us:
he stood, walked toward the stairs,
rested his hand on the railing,
all the while searching closely with his distant stare.
Then slowly he turned away
and sat on one of the steps,
cradling his forehead in his hands.
A convulsive trembling shook his wings.

He is crying, said Lavinia.

The Angel raised his head and listened,
as if he had heard a far-off voice,
a beloved voice calling to him.

Then suddenly he turned.

At first I could distinguish only two moist eyes
shining brilliantly in a blur of white.
Then little by little the shape of his mouth,
the curve of his eyebrows, the angle of his chin
began to take form.

Lavinia bit her lip trying to hold back something:
it could have been a cry, or a name.
But just as she raised her arm,
trembling all over,

just as that cry, that name, was about to break free,
the Angel moved suddenly,
stretched out his hand
and touched her brow.

She collapsed against my chest,
abandoned and inert.
I gathered her in my arms,
carried her down to the foot of the stairs
and laid her on the floor, with her head on my knees.

She had stopped breathing.
A delicate ember still glowed dimly
on the horizon of her lids.
The rest of her face was sinking rapidly into a cold, blue light
shining with the clarity of water and sky.
I turned around, frantic,
searching for the terrible winged child—
but the room was empty and dark.
The house, the garden, the sea
had withdrawn into their glacial night.

I cried out: *Lavinia! Lavinia!*

She lay immobile in my arms,
her face now submerged entirely
within that blue, funereal shadow.
A terrible fury overwhelmed me,
a blind hatred.

I cried out: *Go! Be gone from here, Angel!*
Infernal Angel!

But my voice tumbled dully into the box of silence,
and I felt my hatred crack into icy terror,
a desperate pity.

Don't leave me here, alone!
Angel, take me with you, too!
Don't leave me alone, alive,
in this house!

A beam of moonlight spilled into the room,
and the Angel reappeared, standing by the window,
piercing my heart with his stare:
he had assumed the same eyes, the same mouth,
the same smile as Lavinia.

He moved toward me, came closer,
caressed my forehead with his hand.

Soon, he said,
She will wake up happy.
And remain happy, forever.

And then he disappeared into the luminous air,
leaving me with Lavinia already stirring in my arms,
opening her eyes:
a blissful smile, a smile with no memory,
spreading like the dawn across her lips.

It was the same smile,
that blessed smile with no memory,
which the dead, returning to life,
bring back with them
as a gift.

The Little Hand

(1956)

When he was an infant, Malaparte was sent to live with his wet
nurse, Eugenia Baldi, and her family in a working-class district
of Prato. His mother would come and visit weekly, but he stayed
with Eugenia, her husband, Mersiade, and their sons, Faliero
and Baldo, for the next six years.

For the rest of his life he considered the Baldis, in many
respects, his real family.

When I was a boy,
I loved to be taken by Baldo and Faliero
to visit the rag shops of Prato—
Sbraci's, Campolmi's, Cavaciocchi's, or Calamai's.
And sitting under the feet of busy workers,
we would rummage through heaps of fabric,
finding the most marvelous and unexpected things:
shells, pieces of colored glass,
amber beads, river pearls from India,
stones that seemed precious—
green, purple, turquoise, yellow—
and some the ragmen called *moonstones*—
pale, smooth, and transparent.
Or those red stones which they said would bleed

if you squeezed them hard enough,
so we boys would bite them,
or pinch them between our fingers,
hoping for blood.

Sometimes there were strange dried animals—
they might have been seahorses,
mummified lizards, or mice.
One looked like a fetus with a crushed head.

It was a world unto itself:
the whole city of Prato was a mountainous landscape of rags,
but very few, aside from the ragmen and us boys,
took the trouble to explore those dark continents of cloth.
Occasionally some kids from our street would tag along,
and as soon as we crossed the threshold of the shop,
that smell of rags—dry and dusty,
yet strong and intoxicating as fermenting fruit—
would go to our heads
and trigger a kind of ecstatic snow blindness.

The moment a bale was sliced open,
the rags would pour out
like yellow-red-green-turquoise intestines,
and we would thrust our arms inside this flesh
the color of blood, the color of grass, the color of sky,
rummaging through the swollen stomach,
the hot viscera, of those bundles of rags,
the eyes of our hands searching in that dark wound
for some luminous treasure:
a pearl, a shell, a moonstone.

Then we would plunge headfirst
into those mountains of cloth

the way we might dive into the river's rapids on a summer's day,
slowly dissolving in the deep, sweet swirling odor
of incense, of musk, of clove,
of the perfumes of India,
Ceylon, Sumatra, Java, Zanzibar,
and the fragrances of the South Seas.

One time we found a large-mouthed snake
covered in green and turquoise scales,
smooth and thick as a silken rope.
Another time, a blue tortoise with golden claws
and a Chinese mask of green porcelain.

Then one day we found a woman's hand,
its fingernails lacquered gold:
a little hand, sweet and light as if fashioned of rosewood.

I somehow got the idea
to slip it into my pocket and take it home,
where I hid it under the pillow of the big bed
in which all of us slept:
Eugenia, Mersiade, Faliero, Baldo, and I.
They say the first things to die are the eyes,
and the last are the nails.
Those nails were shiny and sharp, still alive.

That night I couldn't fall asleep,
feverish from the thought of the hand.
I heard it moving under the pillow, bending its fingers,
sinking its nails into the sheets.
Faliero and Baldo, sleeping at the foot of the bed,
had pulled their knees up against their chests,
terrified of the horrible rustling.
I don't know how I ever dozed off,

but I dreamed that the hand was slowly, slowly
crawling out from under the pillow,
slithering along my shoulders,
caressing my throat.

I awoke with a shout
and sat bolt upright, drenched in a cold sweat.
Mersiade gave me a slap to chase away the fright,
but when he saw the little hand,
which had in fact come out from under the pillow,
he turned as pale as wax.
Eugenia, though, seized it with the tips of her fingers
and jumped out of bed.

Calm down! she said.
So much fear for such a little dead hand!

It was the first time it occurred to me
that we might trust the dead more than the living,
that we might have more to fear from the hands of the living
than the hands of the dead.
It was the first time I glimpsed that the dead
may not be foolish, like the living,
but prudent.
And that while being alive exposes you to all sorts of dangers,
forces you to sleep with your eyes open,
if you are dead, you can rest peacefully
with your eyes closed.

Eugenia opened the window, ready to toss the hand outside.
The warm, sweet smell of tomatoes poured into the room.

Don't! It will shrivel up my vines, said Mersiade.

It's your brains that are shriveled! said Eugenia.

And she flung the hand out into the garden,
where we found it the next day,
covered with ants.
They were dragging it slowly through the tomato plants,
toward the hedge of reeds.

We let it go.

It never came back.

Partisans, 1944

(1959)

Malaparte was reassigned as war correspondent to Finland
in early 1942.

I

Around midnight,
we went to buy cigarettes from the partisans.
And where the forest became thicker,
about a mile upriver,
where big blocks of red granite
thrust upward through the grass,
we stopped, and waited.
It was raining.

The rain fell from a high, luminous midnight sky:
one of those transparent Arctic midnights of polished aluminum.
Muffled birdsong filtered through branches
of red pine and white birch,
and the voice of the river rose and fell
like the light from a kerosene lantern.

Suddenly the partisans appeared:
young, blond, tall, thin,
with red cheeks and blue eyes,
impeccably dressed in Allied uniforms:
jackets, overcoats, boots, and gloves
parachuted in from British planes.
We had brought bread, brandy,
reindeer milk, and meat,
in exchange for cigarettes, soap, and toothpaste.

They would hail us in English: *Good morning.*
And we would answer in Finnish: *Hyvää päivää.*
And then all of us would sit on the grass,
around a fire of twigs,
roast a piece of reindeer meat and drink brandy
in silence, without the usual toasts.

We talked little,
and never of the war.
There was a tacit understanding:
never talk of war.
No one wished to be reminded that we were enemies.

After a couple of hours we would get up,
shake hands in silence,
and each would return to his hideout, cabin, or tent.

II

One night, when we arrived at the usual place, we found the partisans
already there, standing among the trees, pale, and silent. One of them,
whom they had left back at camp, needed a doctor.

What is the matter with him? said our captain, Svarstrom.

He is sick, said the Norwegians.

Don't you know what the matter is? said Svarstrom.

No, said the Norwegians.

Svarstrom turned and conferred with his *sissit* in a low voice, then turned back to the partisans.

It would be better if I knew what was wrong with him, said Svarstrom.

We don't know, said the Norwegians.

I don't want to insist, said Svarstrom. *Is he wounded?*

No, he is just sick.

All right, I think we can trust each other. I will send for a doctor.

Not a German, said the Norwegians.

We don't have German doctors in the Finnish army, said Svarstrom.

After a couple of hours, we returned with the doctor, a young medical student from the University of Turku, and found the Norwegians already waiting for us at the usual place. We followed them for a bit, but then they stopped:

The doctor should come alone from here on, one of them said. *And we need to blindfold him.*

No, said Svarstrom. *We are all coming together, and without blindfolds. We are not enemies.*

All right, said the Norwegians, *moving on reluctantly.*

After an hour more, we arrived at a Lapp encampment. Hundreds of reindeer browsed in the fields around the shores of a small lake. The Norwegians took us over to a rough shed, and we entered.

A few partisans were seated around a table, smoking and reading. Over against the wall was an older man, around forty, lying on a cot. He sat up a little as we entered: he was greying, with a short, hard beard. He had staring, clouded eyes, and his hands trembled.

Good morning, he said, in English.

Good morning, I answered.

Everyone else was now standing, looking at us. The doctor came over and sat on the edge of the cot, feeling the man's forehead.

I don't have a fever, said the invalid.

I translated for the doctor, who didn't speak English.

What is the matter with you, then? asked the doctor, taking the man's pulse.

I am afraid.

Afraid of what?

It's a special kind of fear, said the invalid, and then added, smiling: *But not a fear of dying. I am afraid of everything. Especially everything of which people normally are not afraid.*

What did you do, in civilian life? asked the doctor.

A pastor. I was a Lutheran pastor.

When did you begin to feel sick?

The invalid did not answer. He kept silent for a few moments, then said: *I am afraid of God.*

So am I. Everyone is afraid of God. That is not a sickness.

I never said that I was sick.

The doctor leaned closer and examined the man's eyes. *War makes for a cruel sense of humor,* he said.

War is a ridiculous thing, said the invalid. *It's a pretext for men to hurt each other. A ridiculous thing. A children's game. Hurting each other is a children's game.*

I'll give you a sedative, said the doctor.

Thank you, said the invalid, then added, indicating his fellow partisans: *They are also afraid.*

Certainly, we are also afraid, said one of the partisans, smiling.

Yesterday one of them committed suicide, said the invalid.

That happens on our side, too, said the doctor. *It's a question of nerves.*

It isn't nerves. It's something deeper.

Do you have any alcohol? asked the doctor. *I brought some brandy with me. Take a sip now and then, when you feel like it.*

Alcohol is only a way of changing the subject.

That's just the point. Every now and then you need to change the subject. It will do you some good.

If I am sick, then you must be sick, too.

Yes, I am sick. We are all sick. It's the fault of this war.

No. The war is just the symptom of the disease. Are you married?

Yes. With two children.

Then you need to think about killing them. So that they don't get sick as well.

Of course. As soon as the war is over, I will go home and kill my two children.

You think I'm joking, but I'm not. We are preparing a horrible future for our children. Only death can save them.

Here is the sedative, said the doctor, offering the invalid a tube of bromides.

You don't understand anything about me or my illness, said the invalid, pushing the tube away. *I have nerves of steel. Anyway,* he added, *it wasn't for me that you were called, but for someone else. A Russian.*

A Russian? said the doctor.

A Russian partisan. One of the bunch that assassinated the Archbishop of Rovaniemi. He was wounded and we picked him up. I think his leg is turning gangrenous.

A Russian.

I know you hate the Russians, that they are your enemies, but you are a doctor, and it is your duty to help him.

Where is he?

The invalid pulled back the wolfskin that he was using for a blanket, revealing a black, swollen leg, roughly wrapped in bandages.

Ah. He is you, said the doctor, frowning.

Yes, he is me. A Soviet engineer. With a wife and two sons, he added, smiling. *Whom he regrets not having killed before leaving home. Can you do something for the leg?*

I didn't bring my tools with me.

That doesn't matter. You can examine it anyway. And then come back tomorrow.

The leg is gangrenous, said the doctor.

I know, said the Russian, *and it needs to come off. As soon as possible.*

At once, said the doctor. *But I don't have my instruments. I will be back in a few hours.* And he stood up.

Thank you, said the Russian, letting himself fall back onto his cot.

III

We went outside and set off across the forest,
silently following the partisans
through an invisible, luminous rain
in which butterflies traced the liquid outlines
of their wings.

A soft, immense murmuring rose from the grass,
from the bushes, from the trees,
like the buzzing of gelatinous insects.
And the sky curved gently, thickening
as it neared the horizon,
from light green to fleshy pink.
It was a feminine sky, sad and pure.

That sense of northern abstraction:
the impossibility of any heat, smell, or flavor,
the air filled with water and stone,
that thin, smooth odor of the Arctic—
not cold, in fact almost warm,
but deprived of every animal substance,
of every human or vegetable weight—
was the dominant element
in a landscape of trees, water, clouds;
a landscape of distant prospects
modulated more by musical rhythms
than by anything visible to the eye.

One's gaze lost itself
in the green and pink remoteness of Lake Inari
as if in some atonal horizon—
a composition by Schoenberg,
or an abstract sonata by Hindemith.
It was a sky without shadows,
clear yet lightly obscured,
similar to the insides of certain seashells,
where the light is equally reflected from the sea and sky,
creating a separate universe,
secret, pure, intact.

And as seashells capture the reflections of the sandy shore,
of the sky, and of the sea,
and of the voice of the sea,
melting them together in a universe of light and sound
like the reflection of an alternate universe
invisible to the eye and inaudible to the ear,
so this sky seemed a reflection of a universe far from us,
a universe foreign to us, inhuman.
A universe of cruel and impassive abstraction.

In certain hours of the day or night
when the light came to rest
and everything was still, dreamlike,
suspended over an immobile abyss of lakes, forests, rivers,
it seemed then that even the sky had abandoned us,
that over our heads shimmered the void,
the absolute void,
of experimental physics.

Every smell, every color, was extinguished,
and we spent long hours sitting by the shore of the lake,
in that world without smell, without color, without sound;

in that landscape of paper, glass, and luminous shadows,
of transparent stones and trees
where animals moved as they move in dreams:
soundless, colorless, odorless.

Then it began to rain again,
and that diffuse music of Hindemith,
of Schoenberg, would filter down upon us:
music that was as sad, as lonely, and as deep
as a landscape reflected in a mirror.

The partisans said farewell,
and a few miles after crossing the river
we passed the reindeer cemetery:
a multicolored forest of antlers—
brown, green, white—
sprouting from half-buried skulls,
those peculiarly triangular reindeer skulls,
over which the grass had modestly spread
a delicate green cover.

I had often gone there, alone,
to wander through this garden of bones
with its borders of distant sky and lake.
And I would lie down among the forested antlers,
imagining myself wounded
on some remote battleground of history:
one of Xenophon's soldiers
reclining on the banks of the Euphrates;
or a Persian cavalryman abandoned among his dead horses;
or a worker stretched out among broken machinery
after some failed revolution.

And I would rediscover in that grassy garden,
scattered with white bones,

those things which were most Pure,
Precise, Mathematical, and Abstract
about that long-ago bright morning of defeat
on the banks of the Euphrates;
that exact feeling of mechanism
which the neighing of the King's Horses
must have inspired when heard from the far shore;
the voices of the Greek infantry
moving off through transparent air
not yet ripened by the heat of the day,
toward distant mountains hovering blue and white
in the finely etched glass of the sky.

I would rediscover in that reindeer's graveyard,
in that lake shining with the precision of milled steel,
those things which were most Dry,
Arid, Thin, and at the same time Luminous,
about objects and animals:
about polished weaponry, jewels, helmets,
chain mail, strips of leather,
the wheels of wrecked chariots,
the immobile outlines of dead horses and soldiers
lying on the silent, hard-packed battleground.

I would rediscover in that remote horizon—
in which the landscape, slightly shrunken,
appeared and disappeared
like an image reflected in a mirror—
those things which were most Precise,
Essential, Functional, and Logical,
about machines and their disemboweled parts:
dented wheels, transmission belts,
gleaming steel handles, bearings,
gauges, gearings, and crankshafts scattered
on the factory floor

among workers who themselves had been cut loose
with all the essential and definitive precision,
the unchanging precision of a machine.

Those were moments when I felt most detached
from humanity, from all those things
that humanity contributes to life, to nature:
our sensuality and heat, our confusion.
but I did not yet know how to value
that sense of detachment,
that feeling of intimate loneliness,
of distance and difference
from everything that is recognizably human.

IV

I was tired, and threw myself into bed—let the doctor go back to his
partisans without me! It was June, 1944: midsummer in the Arctic. I
turned on the radio—every day brought more battles, more bombardments, more massacres. As soon as I snapped off the switch, the
horrendous smell of blood hovering over Europe began to dissipate.
And the silence, the splendid purity of the Nordic summer, started to
gain the upper hand.

Svarstrom came in to where I was resting and announced: *They
have taken Rome.*

Je m'en fous. I couldn't care less.

It's your country, said Svarstrom.

Je m'en fous.

Don't you care who has taken Rome? asked Svarstrom.

No.

*It was the Allies. They entered Rome last night. The pope blessed the Allied
army from the loggia of St. Peter's.*

Je m'en fous.

I don't understand you, said Svarstrom, shaking his head. And then he added: *They have landed on the coast of France.*

Who?

The Allies. Who else would it be?

I thought it might be the Eskimos.

I don't understand you, said Svarstrom.

A half hour later, a *sissi* came to collect us: the doctor needed help after all. We set out along the trail, and near the river met a pack of wolves. They were loping along through the trees about a hundred yards away, turning to look at us with their red eyes—during the summer when food is plentiful, wolves were not likely to attack us. And in fact they seemed like dogs. Like big dogs, except for the red, glassy eyes which gave their expressions a clear and sad cruelty.

It took a couple of hours to reach the partisan camp, and when we arrived everyone was asleep, even the doctor, who was stretched out on a pile of furs over in a corner, almost underneath the table. Only the Russian was awake, staring at us with his shining, fevered eyes.

The news on the radio is encouraging, said the Russian. *The Allies have taken Rome.*

That's their business, I said.

Don't you care?

It doesn't concern me at all.

That may be stretching it a bit, said the Russian, studying me.

It doesn't concern me at all. If the Germans took Moscow, I couldn't care less.

This war doesn't interest you?

No. Not at all.

The doctor woke up and began going about his business.

You're right, laughed the Russian. *This war is interesting for one reason only: it has murdered Europe.*

Exactly, I said.

But Europe was already dead before it was murdered, said the Russian.

Not everybody knew that, I said. *Now everybody does.*

The doctor asked me to translate for him. It was necessary to amputate, as expected, but the gangrene had progressed, and he wasn't sure if it wouldn't continue to progress even after the operation. He felt it was his duty to try anyway.

All right, said the Russian.

While the doctor prepared his instruments, Svarstrom and I went down to the river's edge: that odor of rotten flesh made me nauseous. It was the smell of Russian winter, 1941.

The shepherds were working around the reindeer stalls and enclosures, gathering sheets of lichen and hanging them on racks to dry in the sun, like the skins of great lizards. Three men returned with salmon they had caught in the river, and the women busied themselves lighting the fires, getting ready to boil the fish in an aluminum kettle.

Two shepherd girls were bathing in the freezing current, swimming slowly with deep, powerful strokes, laughing loudly and calling out to each other. They approached the shore and climbed out of the water, naked. The air was cold, and it was drizzling lightly, but the sun was warm, and they lay down on the grass and closed their eyes. They were young, tall, lithe, with that particular ash-blonde hair that Lapp girls have, their faces covered by thousands of tiny, almost invisible, freckles. A reindeer paused to gaze at them with his round and gentle eyes.

When we reentered the cabin, the doctor was busy washing his hands in a basin. The Russian was unconscious and his amputated leg lay on the table. A heavy, greasy stench emanated from it: the unbearable smell of Naples during the bombardments; of Russian villages along the Don; the stink of Europe. I picked up the leg by its heel.

Let's bury it, I said to Svarstrom.

We took the leg outside, and it seemed to grow heavier, dangling from the tips of my fingers. And to make things worse it was as if that horrible smell was coming from me, from my own flesh. We reached the bank of the river, and Svarstrom began to dig a hole.

The girls were sitting up, smoking their pipes in silence, watching us. They were still naked.

Underneath the topsoil Svarstrom hit a layer of granite, so he moved a few paces away and started to dig again.

The girls began scrubbing themselves, pipes clenched in their teeth, using handfuls of grass soft from the rain. The younger of the two stretched on the tips of her toes to gather some leaves from a birch tree, and used them to scour her long, supple body.

The shovel rang out a second time against granite.

Hurry up. I can't take it much longer, I said. I wanted to let the leg simply drop to the ground, but I didn't, and I can't say why.

Just toss it in the river, said Svarstrom.

I swung the leg back and forth several times and then flung it into the water: it stayed afloat, rotating slowly several times, and then began to slide along with the current.

The girls watched the lazy gyrations of the leg and then started playfully wrestling with each other, laughing softly—almost moaning. They continued for a while, rolling around on grass still shining from the rain, until one bit the other on the shoulder right near the throat.

Meanwhile, the leg caught up against a boulder, disappeared under the water, bobbed to the surface, then finally floated away, leaving horrible ripples in its wake.

The girls stood up, got dressed, and set off toward the village, turning around every so often to look back at us and laugh.

Woman by the Edge of the Sea

(1936)

In June 1933, Malaparte was summoned back to Italy to face charges
of sedition for writing *The Technique of the Coup d'État*, an exposé of
the rise to power of Mussolini, Hitler, and Lenin. He spent his last days
of freedom in Scotland before returning voluntarily to Italy, where he
was sentenced to confinement for five years, of which he served two.

It was past midnight, but the sun
was only now slipping into the sea.
We had just settled down near Flora MacDonald's tomb,
drawn there by views of the distant, coppery Hebrides,
when suddenly the wind shifted, bringing with it
the strong and heady fragrance of northern spring:
that sour-sweet mixture of seaweed and honey.

It had the force of a wave surging onshore,
grabbing me by the scruff of the neck
and flinging me up the grassy slope
before tumbling back in a swirl of foam,
kneading the ocean's seaweed and honey
into the land's thick perfume of milk and wool.

It left my ears buzzing
as if I had just surfaced from a dive.

The sky receded, curving, transparent as vellum;
a silvery fog spread across the sea;
and the grass took on a dark, metallic sheen,
heralding the slow, interminable northern twilight.

I was happy,
full of that indescribable sadness
which is part of our experience of contentment.
Flaminia was there, beside me,
lying in the grass, her white forehead
shining in the brilliant metallic darkness.
She clutched the lapels of her coat
to shut out the sifting sand:
her hands lay like wax
against the rust-colored wool.
The warm breeze had melted them a little,
and a weak reflection
around the white blur of those hands
bled a milky light onto the russet fabric of her coat.

Her silence beside me was alive,
pulsating, arterial:
silence as warm, as perfumed, as fluid
as blood flowing from an open vein.

A lamb on the hills behind us bleated into the humid air,
air that licked the grass like a tongue, reddening it.
Higher up, between the ravines and escarpments,
the restless stags trumpeted their answer,
and that agonized bellowing, as it leapt from rock to rock,
softened into cries of love.

Shepherds patrolled the curving spine of the hills,
searching for the newly born in the brilliant night.
The ewes, still bloody from giving birth, browsed in the grass,
keeping one eye on their lambs,
still moist, hidden in the heather,
blind and soft.
The crescent of the moon shone high in the sky,
as pink as a fingertip.

Flaminia guarded her silence,
hands gathered on her chest,
face turned toward the sea.
And my heart beat strongly:
in a few days we would be back home,
cradled in the dense golden sand
of that familiar red-marble sea.

And I thought:
Perhaps then you will unlock your arms for me, Flaminia,
and your hair will unwind
in the warm resin-flavored waves
of our pine-studded Tyrrhenian coast.

Goodbye, wild Scotland.
Goodbye, immense purple spaces, silken skies,
loving sadnesses of this young spring,
undulating sea, tender and luminous as a prairie,
waves like grass shivering
under the caressing hand of the wind.

I could hear Flaminia breathing softly,
cocooned in her rough wool coat,
her features white in the silvery fog
like a face reflected in a tarnished mirror,

blonde hair coiling onto her shoulders,
swirling around her neck
then snaking down into the grass
heavy and shining as rolls of flaxen silk,
teasing me with a glimpse of ear:
a pink shell half-hidden in honey-colored sand.

Here I am, I thought, *at the summit of my life,*
at the threshold of that ravenous happiness
whose consuming hunger the coming years
will feed first morsels of early regrets,
and then whole carvings of final hopes.

Self-pity swept in on a slow tide.
I was convinced the best of my life had fallen into shadow,
like the cheek of a boy who has slept away the afternoon
by the window.

And it was only then I became aware
of Flaminia hiding her face from me,
turning away that cheek which certainly carried the imprint
of her most secret passions,
and from which, if I could only see it,
I might decipher the mysteries
of her silence and withdrawal.

Juvenile mystery, childish game?
Who knows . . . It was like one of those riddles
of imaginary words and meaningless sounds
which children invent for themselves.
I longed to get up and lie on her shadowed side:
to rest my forehead against that mysterious cheek.
But I was kept back by the fear

of losing myself in the cloud
of that thick, reverberant darkness.

She reminded me of those Etruscan figures
in bas-relief, who rest for eternity
in sepulchers along the Tyrrhenian coast,
one-half of the face held safe against the wall, hidden and pristine,
the other side exposed, etched by time
and the moisture of the tomb . . .

As I was following this trail of thought,
Flaminia raised herself up on her elbows
and gazed off at the distant Hebrides.
Look at me, I tried to say,
but the words died before they left my lips.

I was seized by the sudden and desperate hope
that she would spontaneously turn her face to mine.
And so I stared at her, even more fixedly.
Stared, yet saw nothing more than an ear, an eye,
part of a mouth, a fragment of nose.

Yes, without question, her other cheek,
closely held against the mountain's backdrop of purple heather,
must be marked by secret shadows.
I heard her breathing, then moving,
and finally gently abandoning herself to gravity
as she stretched out on the grass.
Through a trick of perspective
she seemed to have lain along the horizon,
far away upon the crest of the hill,
deep in a panorama of water, mountains, clouds.

She was in, not of, this landscape,
this light, this moment in time:
not part of this shadow now emerging from the sea.
She was foreign to the sadness and savagery of Scotland,
to its prairies and hills,
to the distant islands on the horizon,
to the warm tide of the wind, with its seaweed and honey.
To the whispering of the grass,
to the bleating of the lambs and the bellowing of the stags.
Foreign to the anxious breath of night gradually enveloping us.

I was gripped by a sudden terror:
the fear that Flaminia was now infinitely far away,
unable to hear my faltering voice,
unable to see me,
already blind to everything that concerned me,
my face, my life, my fate.

And I was suddenly overwhelmed,
as with the revelation of a secret truth,
by a formless feeling of death:
by that funereal sweetness which bruises every love,
by that spot of decay which appears after every last kiss,
every goodbye, every separation.

And I thought:
Already my descent has begun,
my hopes are now curled with frost.
Already it is mid-October, and I am wandering in a forest,
a forest that will close around me like a shroud.

Whereas you, Flaminia
you are facing outward to the horizon,

pushed forward toward life
by the light brimming from the cup of the sun.
The sea scarcely feels the impress of your feet,
rosy silver-edged clouds highlight your face,
the blue wing of the sky softens and steadies your step,
the red disk of the East gleams on your shoulders,
and you carry it easily, like an amphora,
your arms raised in a gesture full of carefree grace.

The western horizon had turned the color of flesh,
veined with the dying reflections of sunset.
But already to the east, a restless fog at the edge of the sea
offered a pink forecast of dawn:
the clear northern night was ending before it had begun.
The thrushes sang in the heather,
drunken with happiness,
calling, and then answering
with an intensity which gripped the heart
like the last promises of a dying lover.

The obsessive idea of that mysterious cheek
had become almost painful:
I felt that some useless secret
held half her face in shadow,
just as I was convinced the best part of my life
was already being consumed by that brilliant darkness.

From now on, I will know nothing new about you,
Flaminia, only fragments.
And if I call out to you from the middle of this exile,
oh beloved, from the middle of this landscape
so foreign to your dreams, to your gestures,
to the expressions on your face,

to our dark happiness,
it is because the part of you that is most alive, noble, and pure
is certainly the part of you that is now invisible to me:

Farewell, Flaminia.
I see you now as you first appeared to me:
alone in the sun on the Tyrrhenian shore,
with the entire sky between the pines and the sea
coming to rest on your shining face.
Then, slowly, as you turned toward me,
a great gust of warm air passed across the island,
the sky darkened,
and you were enveloped by a shadow
in whose liquid heart I saw only your face, still shining,
heard nothing but the sighing of the leaves in the wind,
and your breath, woman's breath
whose heart is secret,
always secret.

Red Woman

(1931)

The events described here derived from Malaparte's assignment
to Moscow in early 1929 as foreign correspondent for *La Stampa*.
Malaparte was thirty. Lenin had been dead for five years.
The first of Stalin's show trials had recently concluded with
forty-four prison sentences and five executions.

Tania had promised to take me to Novodevichy Convent Cemetery,
at the tip of a kind of peninsula beyond the suburb of Hamovniki,
embraced on three sides by an ample curve of the Moskva River. The
winter rains had finally stopped, and the earthy, humid smells of spring
sweetened the air, opening up a clear horizon behind the cupolas of
the Kremlin. Sverdlov Square, where we were waiting for the tram,
was less crowded than usual: workers and employees were just leaving
the cafeterias after their lunch break, striding back toward the corner
of Twerskaia Street. Every so often we could hear the distant cries of
the sunflower-seed peddlers who had set up their stalls along the tiled
wall of Kitai Gorod.

A gang of workers in front of the Maly Theater was trying to unload
something from the back of a truck: it turned out to be a monumental
seated sculpture of the playwright Ostrovski, smothered in packing
material and dangling from a pulley by its neck. On the sidewalk

next to the statue, oblivious to the screeching of the winch and the racket of the workers, two cigarette vendors were leaning on their cardboard stands, laughing and gossiping with each other in that loud and lazy Muscovite dialect. It was early in the afternoon, the time of day when gold and green mix playfully with blue, and in the warm air the red-bannered facade of the Bolshoi Theater seemed to be lit with the reflections of a bonfire. A group of deputies was standing among the banners, waiting for the afternoon session of the Soviet Congress: they were from Kinghizi, dressed in that region's large-sleeved red silk robes, black caps, and high, heel-less boots made of soft grey leather. Across the square, near the intersection of Petrovka Street, a platoon of soldiers in grey-green uniforms with flat, short-billed military berets loitered in front of the Hotel Metropol.

Here's the 34, said Tania, as a tram pulled up in front of us. I got on behind her and caught a glimpse of leg: her silk stockings had been mended with threads of various colors. She turned around and smiled, and in the sunlight, her half-closed lids were suddenly red, veined with green.

The tram had just crossed Okhotny Ryad, where the hunters' market used to be, when it unexpectedly jerked to a stop: another group of workers, a few paces from the tracks, were pulling on thick steel cables, shouting in rhythm. They strained backward, feet pointed forward, in a tug-of-war.

Look! said Tania, leaning on my arm. The cables crossed high above the street, which at that point was almost as wide as Sverdlov Square, and wrapped themselves around an old cupola decorated in green and white tiles. A cross, at the top, staggered with each shock.

Every now and then, to catch their breath, the workers let the cables go slack, and the cupola would lurch backward in reprisal, yanking the workers off their feet. A few tiles shook loose and bounced off the roof of the nave, which was almost hidden by the many small houses anxiously crowded around, lending support to the church in its agony. The dull thud of falling plaster was pierced by the terrified screeching of swallows darting like arrows through the dusty air. *Bezprisorni—*

those gangs of ragged homeless boys, orphans of people killed during the revolution—ran around laughing and shouting, chasing each other between the legs of the workers. Some grabbed the ends of the cables and pretended to pull; others raised their arms as if to protect the cupola from collapsing, while the rest held their heads in their hands, wailing, *Oh no!* in mock desperation.

They say there are too many churches in Moscow, said Tania. *One by one they are tearing all of them down.*

She spoke softly, looking at me, and then bent forward to catch a glimpse of the cross glinting in the sunlight, leaning on my arm with all her weight. By now, the tram had inched past the workers and was entering Mokhovaia Street. Further on were the buildings of the University of Moscow, and on the left was the Manege—the famous Moscow riding academy where the neighing of the horses had been cut short during the revolution by the rattle of machine guns.

A few days earlier, something strange had happened: in the morning, Tania had taken me on a circuit of the Museum of the Red Army, Rasumovski's house, various monasteries, and—pride of Bolshevik architecture—the twelve-story Mosselprom building. The afternoon turned hot and Tania felt tired, so we went to an ice-cream shop. It was full of students, workers, state employees, girls with their hair tied back in red handkerchiefs, and a few hopelessly out-of-date older women, with their funny little hats, skirts, and ribbons: ten years after the revolution they were still dressed in the style of their prerevolutionary youth. Everyone turned and looked at us, immediately spotting me as a foreigner.

They think they've seen a bourgeois, I laughed, as we sat down.

If they only knew that I am one, too, whispered Tania. *That I am still a poor bourgeoise.* And then she laughed out loud, leaning back in her chair with eyes half-closed. I was astonished at the sudden change of mood—it was the first time I had seen her like this—but I was particularly struck by the trembling of her right hand. As I leaned forward to touch her, however, someone darted, swift as a lizard, and picked one of the pockets of my jacket. The thief turned out to be a *bezprisorn*, one of those homeless boys from the streets. I was just able to grab his sleeve when a worker, who had been sitting at the next table, loomed over us with his fist raised.

I can't say exactly what happened next—as always in such circumstances, there was a scuffle—but the boy was caught and taken away. I returned the apologetic glances of the other customers with a smile and a shrug, and everyone was soon back in their seats. Tania, though, who had been sitting rigid and pale as a ghost throughout the whole episode, stood up, went over to the man who had hit the boy, and slapped him in the face.

I was so surprised, I forgot what Tania said at the moment of the slap. But afterward she remained standing in front of the worker, repeating over and over: *You shouldn't have hit him. It's not his fault.*

I held her by the arm, more by way of support than restraint. Her voice was low, monotonous, insistent, as children's voices are when they are bewildered by events. Her confusion, along with the behavior of the crowd, would later help me to grasp what had occurred, and what would happen later on.

All the other customers jumped out of their seats and surrounded us, looking at Tania with compassion, as if they understood what she had done and approved of it. I tried to make sense of this, and wondered why the crowd extended their sympathy not only to her, but also to the worker who had been slapped. Everyone was talking loudly, encircling us as if they expected something else to happen.

The only one who hadn't moved, who remained sitting quietly and gave not the slightest sign of surprise or annoyance, was the worker— it was as if Tania's slap had not even grazed him. He was a man in his early forties, small but solidly built—a thick blond beard softened his wide, rawboned face, giving him a patient expression which contrasted with the opaque hardness of his eyes.

He stared firmly back at Tania.

It's wrong to steal, he said in a soft voice, then got up slowly, looked around, and headed for the exit, hesitating at the door. Keeping his back to us, he suddenly raised both fists in the air and repeated loudly: *It's wrong to steal!*

Then he turned slowly, hunched over and frowning, and lifted his eyes to Tania. He fixed her for a moment with a sad, sweet look, smiled, and then turned and left the shop with his head down.

No one said a word. Tania remained perfectly composed. But when the worker's eyes had met hers, and he smiled, she shuddered and her lips blanched. At that moment she seemed so lost and defenseless that I thought it might be a good idea to get her outside.

Let's go, let's go, I whispered, putting an arm around her waist.

Are you as frightened as that? Tania said in Russian, shrugging me off brusquely: *You don't understand anything. You're nothing but a bourgeois.*

And she walked out the door, head tossed back.

Her words, rather than upsetting me, deeply amazed me. And as much as I struggled to figure out their relationship to the events—events which I had witnessed rather than participated in—the truth of the situation would remain hidden to me for some time.

In the days that followed, I held back from discussing any of this, and felt that Tania was grateful for my reserve. I guessed she was hiding something, a secret part of her life, and I didn't have the right to try and unveil it.

Every day thereafter, our friendship became more alive and attentive. I waited for her in the morning near the Iberian Chapel at the entrance to Red Square, under the inscription on the side wall of the Second House of Soviets: *Religion is the opium of the people.* Tania would turn the corner of Nikolskaia Street, smiling, young and agile, full of carefree grace in her usual faded outfit—a straw-colored cotton blouse with a turquoise skirt embroidered in white.

Let's go! she would say, even before *Good morning*—and off we would wander through the streets of Moscow: first into a church or a museum, then a school or a worker's club. At noon we would stop for lunch at a *stalovaia,* a cafeteria full of clerks, workers, students of all nationalities: Chinese, Tartars, Armenians; or at a *duhàn,* one of the many Georgian clubs signposted with some painted Caucasian landscape—the snowy peaks of Kasbek or the glaciers of Elbrus—full of loud voices, gesturing laughter and the smoky air of *sciaslik,* the traditional skewered roast lamb.

In the afternoon if Tania was tired we would stop at a pastry shop or go to a movie; but by the first shadows of evening, when the searchlights had been turned on to illuminate the red flag topping the cupola of the old Senate, I would walk with Tania to the corner of Nikolskaia Street, and would linger on the sidewalk watching until her little ruffled hat disappeared into the crowd.

I didn't even know where she lived. But seeing her come around the corner of Nikolskaia each morning, and then disappearing down Nikolskaia each evening, made me wonder: that street, crossing through Kitai Gorod, ended up at Lubianka Square, where the offices of the G.P.U. secret police were located. I could have followed her to see where she went, but even having these suspicions disturbed me—though there were strange stories circulating around Moscow concerning girls who befriended foreigners.

Where are you coming from? Lubianka? I asked her one morning.

I'm not a spy, she said quietly, looking directly into my eyes. Her voice was clear and sweet, as usual. But for the rest of the day her face was darkened by a slight shadow.

Where did she work? I knew she lived alone in Moscow. How did she support herself?

I'm a clerk in the administration of a theater, she volunteered, before leaving me at the corner of Nikolskaia. But she never said which theater. *I only work in the evenings. It's the usual kind of office work—not as bad as everyone says.*

What right had I to interrogate her about her life? I was a foreigner, a European. *Europe, vielle canaille! Europe, you old rascal!* No foreigner, certainly no bourgeois, could fully grasp the reluctance of a woman in Soviet Russia, even one living at the most basic level, to reveal the miseries and consolations of her life.

Tania seemed to me to come from a good middle-class bourgeois family. She was around eighteen years old, and could have known little of the old Russia, but her knowledge of French, the gaps in her education, even her coquetry, betrayed her origins. She was happy when she could play the part of *une jeune fille bien élevée*—a young well-brought-up girl—and when she could show that she wasn't completely bolshevized (and every time she had to use that word *bolshevized,* she seemed to hesitate).

Tania stood next to me on the crowded 34 with her head on my shoulder. I had put an arm around her waist, and I felt her relax against my side with each jolt of the tram, like a baby falling asleep. She kept her eyes half-closed, breathing slowly, smiling.

Meanwhile, the tram was now traveling down Volchonka Street; large groups of Chinese students drifted through the crowd, overflowing the sidewalks. As we passed the Fine Arts Museum I recalled the painters I had seen there a few days earlier—Titian, Veronese, Francia, Reni, Caracci, Pietro da Cortona. Their work had allowed me, here in the heart of Moscow, to breathe the familiar air of home for a few hours. Parma had never seemed more beautiful as in those two canvases by Bernardo Bellotto.

And now, leaving behind the Chinese university and crossing the piazza which surrounds the Cathedral of the Savior with its five golden domes, the tram slid past the beautiful wooden house built by Domenico Gilardi, which now hosts the Tolstoy Museum.

Look . . . said Tania: the sun was just brushing the bell tower of the Church of the Trinity, flaring its vivid colors.

At each stop, people got on and off the tram with that subdued and hypnotized air which seems appropriate to the suburbs. There were women with babies in their arms, workers with thick blond beards, young proletarians with short hair, pale and apathetic boys with queasy eyes. Everyone looked at us with bored curiosity. By this point, we were on Great Pirogovskaia Street, in the heart of the Hamovniki district, inhabited at one time by the weavers of the czar.

Down one of these side streets, said Tania, *there is a small wooden house where Tolstoy lived for twenty years.*

Shortly thereafter, the tram slowed down, passed in front of the halls of the Polyclinic, and came to a stop in a large piazza.

We had arrived at Novodevichy Cemetery.

Tania walked swiftly down the tree-lined path which flanked the convent wall, keeping the entrance on the right. It was a fortress, really, rather than a convent, judging by the high crenellated walls, the towers, the arrow slits, and not least by the location itself at the tip of a peninsula, protected on three sides by a wide meander of the Moskva and by the swamps which separated it from the river.

This was where Boris Godunov lived for many years as he was plotting to seize the throne; and where Sophia, the stepsister of Peter the Great, was forced to take the veil in 1689. To celebrate this joyful family event, Peter had three hundred of his stepsister's supporters—the *strelzi*—hung by the neck from the trees surrounding the convent—a rare enough spectacle, since *strelzi* when alive were renowned for their ferocity.

Today, to take care of the cemetery—the most famous in Moscow—a few sisters remain, timid ghosts, circulating on tiptoes among the tombs, eyes downcast, mute. But the great resonant halls, the corridors, and the cells of the old convent now echoed with the voices of children, everything brought back to life by the families of workers and bargemen who have been living here since the revolution.

There are the Sparrow Hills, said Tania, pointing to thickly forested hills on the other bank of the Moskva. The clear sky was reflected blue in the river and green in the ponds, the air tasted sweet, refreshed by the spring rain, and the foliage of the trees recast their light on the surrounding grass.

We worked our way down to the edge of a pond, circling along a muddy embankment. Frogs jumped into the water at the sound of our footsteps, surfacing a safe distance away with their heads bobbing, eyeing us warily. Tania laughed and began to run, but the path suddenly veered off from the embankment and became a kind of country road, leading from the shore of the pond to some railway tracks, where a freight train was puffing away; the engine gave a shove to a line of cars, which detached and rolled silently down the track, the engine then chasing them, catching up, making contact with a clang, and pushing them off again in a cloud of steam, only to restart the whole game a hundred meters down the track.

A bit further along we caught a glimpse of the Sparrow Hill train station—a little suburban station, deserted and forgotten at the tip of the peninsula between the ponds and the river. Closer by, two boys were rooting around in the pond's black silt, looking for earthworms. A thick muddy perfume hovered in the air, and when we walked past, the boys looked up, curious and annoyed. They kept their eyes on us for a stretch, until the road suddenly bent to the right, disappearing into an underpass.

The tunnel was low and short, and the sound of the freight train vibrated through the brick walls with a deep rolling thunder. We had scarcely entered when ten mounted Cossacks trotted into the tunnel from the other end, horseshoes clattering loudly. The horses jostled nervously against each other, pawing the ground, then moved forward shaking their bridles. Tania, with her back to the wall, stretched out a hand to pat their glistening, sweaty rumps. She turned, laughing, and said something to me, but it was lost in the racket. One of the Cossacks leaned over as he passed and brushed our faces with a handful of grass, laughing as he did so, delighted as a child.

These were no longer Cossacks the way we remember them—with cartridge belts crossed over their chests, kaftans, wide funnel sleeves, and tall astrakhan *sciapke* pulled down to their ears—now they had yellow-grey uniforms with short-billed caps in the English style: handsome tanned boys, athletic and limber, with black eyes and gleaming teeth in taut and dusky faces. Suddenly the boom of hooves and voices fell away, dissipating into the yellow sunny air. The Cossacks turned to smile at us with one hand on the croup of their horses before disappearing around a bend in the road.

We emerged out into the open, and were confronted by a wide expanse of grassland. The road led directly down to the river.

Let's go back, said Tania.

Facing us on the other side of the river were the Sparrow Hills—the Vorobyovy Gory—thickly forested with luminous foliage. It was from the top of these hills that Napoléon got his first view of Moscow. White clouds sprouted behind the trees, and a light breeze silvered the grass.

Let's go back, whispered Tania, clutching my arm.

The two boys were still at the edge of the pond, bent over, rummaging with their hands in the black silt. We walked in silence along the muddy embankment, returning toward the convent cemetery where Chekhov lay.

On the other side of those walls, said Tania softly, indicating the newer section of the cemetery, *are the tombs of Scriabin and Kropotkin.*

A nun moved silently among the crosses, and a few older couples were seated here and there on the stone benches which flanked the graves of every enclosure.

I'm cold, whispered Tania. A slight shiver fluttered across her pale features, and a sudden fatigue, almost sleep, pressed against her green-veined eyelids. I put my arm around her waist and pulled her closer to me, but she shrugged me off with a glare. We wandered into the enclosure of a tomb, and stayed there a while, sitting silently side by side on the stone bench. The name *von Meck* was chiseled into the marble: I recalled that a few days earlier, a von Meck, the director of the Soviet railway system, had been executed by the G.P.U. [*Translator's note: Nikolai von Meck was executed on May 23, 1929, aged sixty-six. His mother, Nadezhda von Meck, had been Tchaikovsky's principal benefactor for thirteen years.*]

I'm cold, whispered Tania. Her eyes were now half-closed, and her hands trembled in mine. I gathered her in my arms and grazed her hair with my lips, searching for her mouth.

You are all the same, she laughed, disentangling herself. Her eyes were brimming with tears.

It was only later, thinking about the times we spent together—Tania's sudden aberrations, her mercurial moods, her proud and impatient sensibility—that I could understand the reasons for her strange demeanor. She never granted me much more than a smile; her secrets, her infrequent spontaneities, her dreams and worries always had an underlying tone of resentment and suspicion.

You would certainly never say that there was attraction between us, but neither was it simple friendship. How many times had I felt in her glance that opaque sadness which is the presentment of love!

With me, Tania was free to enact the part of the *jeune fille bien élevée,* and I felt she was sincere when she shrugged off my embraces. She had given herself over to this game, and now she believed in it almost instinctively. With me, she was able to breathe for a few hours the air of that existence she had never known—she was still a child at the beginning of the revolution—and which she could never have known. Her harmless game gave her the illusion of living in an atmosphere which was dead and gone, in a world swept away forever.

Every day, for a few hours, she plunged into this dream of her origins and education, able to show to a foreigner, a European, that in the ruins of the moral and social world she inhabited—proletarian Russia—she had been able to hold intact the principles and standards of a proper bourgeois upbringing.

And every day, on waking from this dream, she would feel again, as if for the first time, the world of bourgeois morality, already dead around her, beginning to collapse inside her. Insidious doubt had entered her spirit, infecting her, like all the young people of her generation. And the effects of that disease, every so often, would flourish suddenly and unexpectedly in her behavior, and she would then blush as if she had revealed to me, through some involuntary gesture, a secret wound. She blushed as if she were guilty.

I will never forget the words and looks with which she sometimes greeted my casual observations about things, about the customs and the spirit of revolutionary Russia. One day, we had gone to Lenin's mausoleum, built at the base of the Kremlin wall in Red Square. The embalmed corpse lay there in front of us in its glass sarcophagus: Lenin's extraordinarily white face, sprinkled with freckles, ended in a pointed red beard. And given the white glaze of the flesh and the bright color of the beard you might think it was a wax mask rather than a human face.

From the portraits of him, I thought that Lenin's beard was black, I observed. I hadn't said anything particularly outrageous, but Tania looked at me askance.

This corpse will kill you too, she said with an edge to her voice.

I was aware, from her subsequent silence, that she regretted this outburst, as if afraid of having revealed a secret. I remembered the episode of the *bezprisorni,* and the slap she had given the worker who had caught the thief. And I remembered when I had talked to her about the execution of von Meck, which had happened a few days earlier, and of the terror throughout Russia elicited by the initials G.P.U.

Only traitors need to be afraid of the G.P.U., she answered flatly, turning away. But I understood that those words had just popped out of her mouth, and I pretended not to have heard them.

I can still see her, poor Tania, in the Novodevichy Cemetery, her eyes brimming with tears, but only now can I understand her secret anguish, and the purity of those tears.

After returning from Novodevichy that evening, and leaving Tania as usual at the corner of Nikolskaia, I strolled over to the Stanislavski Theater, where they were performing a comedy by Bulgakov: *Days of the Turbins.* The theater was full—workers and clerks dressed as peasants *à la mode de Tolstoy,* girls with short hair and faded blouses, Communist Youth Party members in uniform, with their narrow English-style belts, proud and reserved, women of the people with their hair tied back in red bandanas, soldiers scattered in groups here and there, government officials with freshly razed craniums, dignified and courteous.

It was hot, and a heavy atmosphere weighed on the attentive and silent crowd. Between acts, the audience spilled out into the street to smoke, gather around the lemonade stands, and stretch their legs, talking and laughing in subdued voices.

At the end of the last act—when the chords of the *Internationale* rose from backstage and the marching of the victorious Red Army entering Kiev vibrated under the windows of the Turbin household, I hurried for the exit before the final curtain and walked slowly toward Sverdlov Square.

The season of the white nights had already begun—those warm and luminous nights of the north, when the day stretches until dawn. The streets of the city were immersed in an eclipse-like light, and in the still air, perfumed and tepid, the trees were made of silver.

Halfway along Teatralniy Proyezd, the wide street connecting Sverdlov Square to Lubianka, the noise of an argument made me look up: a small crowd had gathered at the corner of Rozhdestvenka Street, in front of the entrance to a *stalovaia*. The circle of onlookers would alternatively widen out to give more space to the argument, and then tighten up as if a hundred hands were reaching out to grasp and divide them. Someone inside the *stalovaia* was singing, accompanied by an instrument, and the song helped to give a *cadenza* to the shouts and laughter, a dance rhythm to the confused movement of the crowd.

What's going on? I asked a cigarette vendor, who was staying carefully at a distance, with his cardboard case slung around his neck.

It's two prostitutes fighting each other, he answered, laughing.

I moved closer, pushing my way forward, and there, panting in front of me, disheveled, their clothes torn, faces flushed, two girls were scuffling and shouting hoarse insults at each other.

Tania! I shouted.

At the sound of my voice, Tania turned, freed herself from the grasp of her adversary, took a few steps back and stopped, pale as a ghost.

Tania! I shouted.

Tania lifted her arms, and in that silence, in an unforgettable voice, pleading and desperate, she cried out:

Bourgeois! Bourgeois! Tu ne comprends rien. You don't understand anything, bourgeois!

And then she disappeared, buried in the crowd, which quickly closed around her with a burst of laughter.

Empty Sky

(1958)

In 1956, Malaparte traveled to China. He was one of the first
Western journalists to interview Mao after the Korean War.

The Chinese cannot imagine animals without paws.
All animals have them:
In China even snakes and dragons
have four paws.

And in Chinese theater the human face
is always painted or masked:
Emperors, Heroes, Angels, Devils,
everyone has a mask.
The only ones with naked faces
are the Poor.

And Chinese artists never paint the sky.
Where we put blue or black
they leave the canvas bare.
The Sun and Moon hang round and red
in canvas skies,

without clouds, without stars,
for company.

But sometimes a bird flits across this bare canvas,
this empty sky.

The Gun Gone Mad

(1944)

This is a "missing" chapter from Malaparte's book *Kaputt*. It appears
in the Italian and French editions but for unknown reasons was not part
of the English translation by Cesare Foligno, published by E. P. Dutton
in 1946. The events described concern Hitler's Unternehmen Strafgericht
(Operation Punishment): a four-day carpet bombing of Belgrade without
a declaration of war. It was one of the first terror bombings of a civilian
population in the Second World War, resulting in anywhere from six
thousand to twenty-four thousand deaths. It precipitated the collapse
of the Kingdom of Yugoslavia and yielded Nazi hegemony over south-
eastern Europe in preparation for Operation Barbarossa, the attack on
the Soviet Union. The commander of the Luftwaffe formations involved,
General Löhr, was tried for war crimes by a Yugoslavian military court
and executed in 1947. The Italian envoy described here, Francesco G.
Mameli, shares the same surname as Goffredo Mameli (1827–1849),
who composed the lyrics to the Italian national anthem, known everywhere in Italy as Inno di Mameli (Mameli's Hymn).

When the bombing of Belgrade began, Mameli, the Italian envoy to
the Kingdom of Yugoslavia, called out to his dog, a beautiful three-
year-old red setter.

Spin, let's go, quick!

Spin was curled up in a corner of the ministry office, right underneath the portraits of the pope, the king, and Mussolini, as if asking for their protection. He did not even dare to get up and cross the room to his master, who was standing in the doorway.

Spin, let's go, quick! We have to go down into the shelter.

From the unusual tone of Mameli's voice, Spin knew that there was some reason to be really afraid, and he began to whine, to dribble on the carpet and look around with a bewildered expression in his eyes.

Spin was a handsome purebred English dog and he had one passion in life: the hunt. Mameli often took Spin hunting in the woods and on the hills around Belgrade, along the shores of the Danube or those little islands in the river between Pančevo and Zemun. He would take a gun down from the wall, swing it on his shoulder and call out: *Spin, let's go!* Spin would bark and jump with joy, and as he trotted along the corridor where Mameli kept all his guns, cartridges, and beautiful English leather game bags he would look around and wag his tail.

But that morning, as soon as the bombing began, Spin was seized by fear. The crash of the bombs was dreadful. The building of the Italian Legation, not far from the old Royal Palace, was shaken to its foundations by terrible explosions: flakes of plaster fell from the walls, long cracks appeared in the partitions and ceilings.

Let's go, Spin! Quick!

It was seven twenty in the morning of April 6, 1941—Palm Sunday. Spin made his way downstairs to the bomb shelter with his tail between his legs, whimpering and dribbling on the stairway. He had first passed through the corridor and looked up at the walls: the guns were all in their places. These stupendous blasts, therefore, were not gunshots at all, but something abnormal, absolutely outside of humanity, outside of nature.

The shelter was a simple wine cellar with a tamped-earth floor; there hadn't been time enough to prop up the rafters or to reinforce the vault with armor. A dingy, dusty light filtered in from a small opening at street level. On rustic shelving along the walls were flasks of Chianti, bottles of French wine, whisky, cognac, and gin. Friulian *prosciutti* from San Daniele hung from the ceiling alongside salami from Lombardy. It was just a wine cellar, a real mousetrap; one little bomb would have been enough to bury the whole staff of the legation, along with Spin.

The earth staggered, as if from the shock of an earthquake, and houses knocked against each other. You could hear the horrendous clatter of walls collapsing, the smash of windowpanes hitting the sidewalk, and the cries of terror, weeping, calls for help, curses, and the bellowing of people driven mad in full flight. An acrid smell of sulfur began to infiltrate the wine cellar along with smoke from the explosions and fires. The bombs were falling on Terazije, on Monument Square, on the old Royal Palace. Vehicles of all descriptions raced through the streets in columns, loaded with generals, ministers, dignitaries of the court, high functionaries. Terror had gripped the civil and military authorities and they were all now abandoning the capital. By ten o'clock in the morning the city was left to fend for itself. And then the looting began.

The mob, which had been swollen by gypsies from Zemun and Pančevo, ripped the corrugated-iron shutters from the stores and then ran upstairs, ransacking people's homes. Citizens and looters fought in the streets, on the stairways of the palaces, on the landings, inside the apartments. The rattle of gunfire could be heard coming from the direction of Terazije. On Monument Square, the Royal National Theater was burning.

The pastry shop which faced the theater on the other side of the square had collapsed. It had been a Turkish bakery famous all over the Balkans for its aphrodisiac specialties. The roaring crowd scavenged through the rubble, vying ferociously for the precious sweets. Disheveled women, their faces incandescent, streaked the air with obscene laughter as they stuffed themselves with those fleshy confections.

Spin heard all this—the explosions, the cries of terror, the laughter, the crackling of fires—with his ears drooping, tail between his legs, moaning. He was curled up between Mameli's feet, dribbling on his master's shoes.

By the middle of the afternoon the thunder of the bombs had gradually drifted away, and Mameli and the functionaries of the legation climbed the stairs to the ground floor. But Spin refused to leave—they had to bring food down to him, there in the darkness of the smoke-filled wine cellar.

Spin's world had collapsed. From the ministry office you could hear his moaning during the occasional moments of silence. Something horrible, even supernatural, must have taken place, and Spin could not make sense of it.

The bombing is over, Mameli would say to him each time he went down to the wine cellar. *You can come upstairs now, the danger has passed.*

But Spin didn't want to leave. He wouldn't touch his food, looking at it with suspicious eyes, those shy and imploring eyes of a dog who is now afraid of being betrayed by the hand of his master. No human or natural law existed any more. The world had collapsed.

Around four in the afternoon of that same day, when Mameli was just about to go down to the shelter to try once again to persuade Spin that the danger was over—that from now on everything was back to normal, to the usual traditional order—he heard a distant buzz high in the sky over Pančevo. The first bombs fell somewhere near Miloša Velikog, huge bombs which the *Stukas* hammered down into the roofs like someone would pound a nail, with a single, scorching, precise, violent hammer-stroke.

And the city shook to its foundations, with howling crowds pouring into the streets. But every so often, between one explosion and the next, there would be a great silence: everything would hold its breath, immobile, death all around. It was exactly how the silence of nature will be when the Earth itself is dead—that extreme, immense sidereal silence of the Earth when it is cold and dead, when the destruction of the world will finally have been achieved.

Then suddenly another horrendous explosion would uproot trees and houses, and the sky would collapse upon the city with a clap of thunder.

Minister Mameli and the functionaries of the legation had gone back down into the shelter, and now they were seated, a little pale, on some chairs that the staff had arranged around a table in the middle of the wine cellar. All that could be heard, between one explosion and the next, was the whining of Spin, snuggled between the legs of his master.

It's the end of the world, said the second secretary, Prince Fulco Ruffo.

It's really hell, said Minister Mameli, lighting a cigarette.

All the forces of nature are arrayed against us, said the first secretary Guidotto. *Even nature has gone mad.*

There's nothing to be done, said Count Fabrizio Franco.

The only thing we can do is imitate the Romanians, said Minister Mameli. *Tutun și răbdare—smoke and wait.*

Spin listened to this conversation and knew very well that there was nothing else to be done. *Tutun și răbdare,* yes. But wait for what? Minister Mameli and the functionaries of the legation might know exactly what they were waiting for, sitting pale and nervous, smoking one cigarette after the other. If at least one of them would let slip the word which would reveal to Spin the mystery of this agonized waiting!

The darkness in which he found himself, along with the events of this terrible day and the mystery of this waiting, added an anxiety to the terror of those enormous bomb blasts, an anxiety worse than any uncertainty. Not that Spin was a timid dog. Spin was a brave English dog, a purebred, raised at the best kennel in Sussex. He was afraid of nothing, not even of war: Spin was a hunting dog, and everyone knew that war was a hunting party where men were both hunters and prey: a game in which men, armed with guns, hunted one another. Spin was not afraid of gunfire: he would have gone head-on against an entire regiment. Gunshots made him jump for joy. They were an essential component of nature, a fundamental element of the world, of his world. Without gunshots, what would life be? What would life be without those long runs across the meadows and the scrublands, through the hills beyond the Danube and the Sava, following a scent taut as a wire across the fields and through the woods, running along that scent like an acrobat balancing on a steel wire.

When Mameli's shot would snap out dryly in the clear thin air of the morning—or would spread out softly with a slight trembling in the grey spider's web of an autumn rain, or rebound happily across snowy plains—the order of nature was revealed in its perfection. It only took the sound of a gunshot to give the final touch of perfection to nature, to the world, to life.

During the long winter nights when Mameli would sit by the fire in the library poring over the pages of some book with a short pipe clenched in his teeth, Spin would curl up at his master's feet dreaming of the dry *crack* of the gun and the tinkle of the glassy morning air. He would lift his eyes every so often to the old Turkish gun hanging on the wall beside the door, and wag his tail.

It was a flint-action shotgun encrusted with mother-of-pearl that Mameli had bought for a few *denari* from a junk dealer in Monastir. It had without doubt fired at the Christian soldiers of Prince Eugene of Savoy, at the Hungarian and Croatian cavalry galloping through the fields of Zemun. An old, faithful war gun, which had done its duty, completed its mission, contributed to maintaining the traditional order of nature, and had, in its long-ago youth, given the final touch to the perfection of the world on that day when its dry *crack* had broken the glass of the morning and a young *uhlan* had fallen from his horse, down there in Zemun, in Novi Sad, in Vukovar. Spin was not "a son of a gun" but he could not conceive of a world without guns. As long as the voice of the gun reigned supreme, nothing could disturb the order, the harmony, the perfection of nature.

But the brutal cacophony which had, that morning, caused the world to crumble was not—could not be!—the voice of the gun. It was an unfriendly voice never heard before: a new, frightful voice. Some horrible monster, some foreign god, had toppled the Kingdom of the Gun, had overthrown forever that familiar god who, until this day, kept the world balanced in order and harmony. The voice of the gun would remain forever silent, conquered by this savage booming.

And the picture of Mameli—such as it appeared to Spin's imagination at these desperate moments of denatured nature and a ruined world—was the picture of a poor little man, stooped, grizzled and pale, who limped with an empty game bag through barren fields and ashen woods—and on his shoulder was a gun, useless and silent, vanquished.

But suddenly a terrible idea broke into Spin's thoughts: perhaps that horrible voice . . . perhaps that savage voice really was, from now on, the new voice of the gun. Perhaps the gun, infected by a rabid madness, was now racing through the streets, the fields, the woods, the riverbanks, ravaging nature with its new, horrible, frenzied voice.

At this thought, Spin felt his blood run cold. A picture of Mameli, armed with this terrible gun, hovered menacingly before his eyes: Mameli slipping a cartridge into the barrel, raising the gun, placing the stock against his shoulder, pressing the trigger. A horrible thunder bursts from the mouth of the gun. A tremendous explosion shakes the city to its foundations, deep chasms open up in the earth, the houses knock against each other then collapse with an enormous clatter, kicking up immense clouds of dust.

In the wine cellar everyone was silent, pale and sweating. Someone began to pray. Spin closed his eyes and abandoned his soul to God.

That same day I was in Pančevo, just outside of Belgrade. The immense black cloud which had risen over the city seemed, from this distant vantage point, to be the slowly beating wing of an immense vulture, blanketing the city with its vast bulk. The setting sun struck it sideways, and it glistened with soot and blood—the wing of a mortally wounded vulture, struggling to lift off, tearing the sky with its rough feathers.

Over there, above the city huddling on its wooded hill at the end of a vast plain crisscrossed by lazy yellow rivers, flocks of *Stukas* pounced relentlessly, beaks outstretched, screeching horribly, and with their beaks and claws they tore apart the white houses, the high palaces sparkling with glass, the roads that fanned out across the plain from the margins of the suburbs. Tall fountains of earth gushed along the banks of the Danube and the Sava. Above my head was a continuous roar, an incessant screeching of metal wings glistening in the last light of day. The horizon pulsated deeply, like a savage tom-tom. Gleams of distant fires surged here and there across the plain.

Straggling Yugoslav soldiers wandered through the countryside, and German patrols could be seen snaking along the ditches, searching the fields of reeds and rushes at the edges of the ponds along the Tamiš.

It was a soft, pale evening . . .

A swollen moon rose slowly over the hills
along the rim of the horizon.
The water of the Danube sparkled.
And while I watched that moon slowly rising
into the sky—a sky as pink as a baby's fingernail—
a mournful chorus of dogs leapt into the air.

No human voice can equal the voice of the dog
in expressing universal sadness.
No music, not even the purest,
can equal the voice of the dog
in expressing the sadness of the world.

Held at the edge of a long sustained breath,
the notes were modulated, tremulous,
suddenly breaking into a sob, high and clear.

They were hopeless appeals,
distressed calls from the marshes,
the woods, the thickets,
the fields of reeds and rushes
where the wind spent itself
with a murmuring shiver.

Dead bodies floated
on the water of the ponds,
and from the carcasses of horses
abandoned along the road,

flocks of crows gilded by the moon
rose heavily into the air
with a silent beating of wings.

Packs of hungry dogs
prowled around the villages—
some ruined house still smoking like an ember.
They passed at a gallop—
that tight and heavy gallop
of frightened dogs—
turning their heads from side to side,
jaws open, eyes red and glittering.
And from time to time
they would stop to howl mournfully
at the moon.

A fat yellow moon,
soaked with sweat
slowly rising into the pink fingernail sky
cast a soft diaphanous light
over ruined and deserted villages,
fields and roads scattered with the dead,
and the white city in the distance,
covered with that black wing of smoke.

I was forced to remain three days in Pančevo. Then we finally began
to move, crossing the river Tamiš and the peninsula which the Tamiš
creates where it flows into the Danube. We were obliged to stop for
another three days on the banks of that great river directly opposite
Belgrade, beside two towers of twisted iron—all that remained of the
bridge dedicated to King Petar II.

Scorched roof-beams gyrated in the rapid yellow current of the
Danube, tangled up with mattresses and the carcasses of horses, pigs,
cattle. There in front of us on the opposite riverbank lay the city in

its agony, suffused with the thick perfume of spring. Clouds of smoke billowed from the railroad terminal.

Finally one day near sunset, Captain Klingberg and four soldiers crossed the Danube in a small boat and occupied Belgrade. Then we ourselves were allowed to cross the immense river, protected by the solemn gestures of the *Feldwebel* of the Grossdeutschland Division, who was directing the river traffic. He stood apart, essential and purely abstract, like a Doric column erected on the embankment of the Danube, sole arbiter of the enormous movement of men and machines.

We entered the city near the railroad station, at the bottom of Prince Pavle Avenue.

A green wind . . .

A green wind ruffled the leaves of the trees.
It was already near sunset,
the last light of day drizzled down
like extinguished cinders
from a grey and opaque sky.
I passed motionless taxis and trams
full of bodies.

Enormous cats, squatting on cushions
next to dead bodies already livid and swollen,
stared at me with slanted phosphorescent eyes.
A yellow tom followed me
for a while, meowing as I walked on a brittle carpet
of splintered glass.

Now and then I met some passerby
who would skim along the walls,
looking around suspiciously.
No one answered my questions,

staring at me with strangely white eyes,
moving on without glancing back.
The expression on their unwashed faces
was not fear, but enormous surprise.

There was just a half hour until curfew. Terazije was deserted. In front of the Hotel Balkan, a bus had stopped at the edge of a bomb crater, full of dead passengers. On Monument Square, the Royal National Theater was still burning. It was an evening of thick translucent glass: a milky light bathed the ruined houses, the empty streets, the abandoned vehicles, the trams frozen in the middle of their tracks. Here and there throughout the dead city, gunshots echoed out, dry and malignant.

It was already dark when I finally arrived at the Italian Legation. The building at first glance seemed intact; then, bit by bit, the eye discovered the broken window-glass, the torn blinds, the scorched walls, the roof lifted askew by an immense explosion.

I entered, climbed the stairs: the interior was lit with little oil lamps scattered around on the furniture, like the lamps used for sacred icons. Shadows danced on the walls.

The minister of Italy, Mameli, was in his office, bent over some papers, his gaunt face immersed in the yellow halo of two candles. He stared up at me, shaking his head as if he didn't believe his eyes.

Where did you come from, he asked. *From Bucharest? Through Timisoara and across the Danube? And how the devil did you do that?*

He told me about the frightful bombardment and massacre. *There's a lot to be ashamed about,* he said, *being allied with the Germans.*

They had lived through days of agony, easy prey for the looters, locked in the legation while they waited for German troops to occupy the city. A thousand-kilo bomb had exploded right on the other side of the garden wall. *But thanks to God,* he said, *we all got through it, not even an injury.*

I watched him as he spoke: he had two livid circles around his eyes, a haggard face, and eyelids red from insomnia. Mameli was a small man, thin, and a little stooped. For many years he had walked with a cane, limping from a war wound, and even now he trailed one of his legs slightly. How long had I known him? More than twenty years. He was a good and honest man, Mameli, and I liked him a lot. War offended him as if it were an insult to his honor, to his Christian feelings. Suddenly he stopped talking and put a hand over his face.

Let's get something to eat, he said, after a long silence.

Around the table all the faces were pale, sweaty, unshaven. For many days Mameli and the functionaries of the legation had lived like a garrison in a besieged fort. Now the siege was over, but there still was no water, gas, or electricity. The staff were dressed impeccably, yet there was still something frightened in their sleepy faces. The light from the candles danced in the crystal glasses, the silverware, the white linen. We ate a bowl of soup, a little cheese, an orange. After dinner, Mameli took me into his office and we started talking.

Where is Spin? I asked.

Mameli gave me a sad look, and in his eyes there was a shadow of shame.

He is sick, he answered.

Oh, poor Spin. What's wrong?

Mameli blushed, and he replied clumsily, averting his eyes: *I don't know what it is. He is just sick.*

It will turn out to be nothing serious.

Yes, of course, it's just some small thing, Mameli answered quickly. *It won't turn out to be anything serious.*

Do you want me to take a look at him?

No, thanks, Mameli answered, blushing. *It's better to leave him alone.*

Spin and I are friends, he would like to see me.

Yes, certainly, he would like to see you, said Mameli, bringing the glass of whisky to his lips, *but perhaps it is better to leave him alone and quiet.*

It would do him good to see an old friend, I said, standing up. *Where is he? Let's go and say good night to him.*

You know how Spin can be, said Mameli without getting up from his chair. *He doesn't like to be cared for when he is sick. He doesn't like doctors or nurses. He wants to get better by himself.* Meanwhile he took the bottle of Johnnie Walker and offered it, smiling: *A little more whisky?*

Spin isn't sick, I said. *He is angry at you because you don't take him hunting anymore. You've gotten lazy, and have been for some time. You just want to take it easy, you never leave the house. A sign of old age. Isn't it true that you've gotten lazy?*

It's not true, said Mameli, blushing. *It's not true. I take him hunting every week. We have had great adventures lately. We even went to Fruška Gora just a month ago and camped out for three days, just before my wife left. Spin isn't angry with me. I told you that he was sick.*

Let's go see him, then, I said, heading toward the door. *Where is he?*

He's in the wine cellar, answered Mameli, lowering his eyes.

In the wine cellar?

Yes, in the wine cellar. In the bomb shelter, I mean.

In the bomb shelter? I said, staring at Mameli.

I tried everything, he doesn't want to come up, answered Mameli, keeping his eyes averted. *He's been down there in the bomb shelter for almost ten days.*

He doesn't want to come up? Then we should go down.

And so we went downstairs, taking a kerosene lantern. Spin was curled up in the darkest, most secret corner of the wine cellar, on a pallet made of sofa cushions: at first I saw a soft and frightened light in his clear eyes, then I heard the beating of his tail on the cushions. Stopping at the last step on the stairway, I asked Mameli in as quiet a voice as possible:

What the devil is wrong with him?

He's sick, answered Mameli.

All right, but what the devil is it?

He's afraid, said Mameli softly, blushing.

Spin really had the appearance of a dog crushed by fear, by an enormous fear. And added to the fear was a feeling of shame. As soon as he saw me and recognized me by my smell and my voice, he lowered his ears and hid his muzzle between his paws, looking up at me from below—all the while with his tail wagging slowly, as dogs do when they are ashamed of themselves. He had lost weight; his ribs showed through his skin, his side was caved in, and his eyes were watery.

Oh, Spin! I cried, in a tone of compassion mixed with reproach.

And Spin stared at me with his imploring eyes, then stared at Mameli with disappointment, and now I understood that Spin was trapped in a tangle of feelings: fear, disappointment, regret, and even a little self-pity—yes, a little self-pity.

It's not just fear, I said. *It's something else.*

What else? said Mameli eagerly, almost joyfully.

It's not just fear, I said. *There is another emotion—darker and deeper. I have the suspicion, and the hope, that it isn't only fear. Fear is something disgraceful. No, it isn't only fear,* I said.

And as Spin listened to me, he cocked his ears.

You are taking a great weight off my heart, said Mameli. *There have never been cowards in my family. This would be the first case of cowardice in my family. We Mameli have always been brave, and it would be a great sadness for me if Spin was unworthy of the name he carries, the name of Mameli.*

Oh, I am sure that Spin is worthy of the traditions of your family. Isn't that right, Spin? "You are a brave dog, aren't you?" I said to him in his native language, stroking his forehead. Spin looked at me, wagging his tail. Then he looked at Mameli, eyes brimming with disappointment, pity, regret, with a look full of affectionate reproach.

Good night, Spin, I said. Mameli and I went back upstairs to the office and sat down in the armchairs next to the cold fireplace. We stayed there a while, not saying anything, just smoking and drinking. Every now and then Mameli would look at me and sigh.

Tomorrow morning, I said, *you'll see that Spin will be cured. I have a marvelous medicine.* I stood up and Mameli took me to my room. He said good night with a sad voice, and I listened as he walked away with his light step, a little unsteadily, and it seemed to me that he was limping more than usual.

My bed was a sofa in a lounge off the dining room. I took off my boots and threw myself onto the cushions, but couldn't get to sleep. Through the big glass door separating the lounge from the dining room

I glimpsed the glasses and the crystal decanters, the porcelain, the silver, gleaming softly in the shadows.

The sofa was in a corner, underneath a painting which represented the biblical story of Joseph and Potiphar's wife. The mantle of the chaste Joseph was a beautiful red wool, soft and warm. I didn't have anything to cover myself except for my overcoat, which was soaked with rain and smeared with mud.

And in the gesture of the lascivious wife of Potiphar I flattered myself to see maternal compassion and feminine concern, almost as if she was moved not by the impure desire of a sinner but by the good and honest intention to take the mantle from Joseph and let it fall on my shoulders.

The footsteps of the German patrols echoed gloomily in the deserted street. Around one in the morning, someone knocked at the door of the Bulgarian Legation on the other side of the street.

Quiet, don't make any noise, I said, at the edge of sleep. *Don't wake poor Spin.*

But at that moment, Spin was asleep. "You are a brave dog, aren't you?" Suddenly my fatigue got the upper hand, and I tumbled head-long into sleep.

In the morning I said to Mameli: *Take down your hunting gun.*

Mameli went into the corridor and took the gun off the wall, cracked it open and blew into the barrels.

And now let's go and get Spin, I said.

We went downstairs, crossed the threshold of the wine cellar, and as soon as Spin saw Mameli with the gun in his hands he lowered his eyes, hid his muzzle under his paws, and began to whimper softly, with the voice of a baby.

Let's go, Spin, I said.

Spin stared at the gun with wide-open eyes and began to tremble.

Come on, Spin, let's go, I repeated in a tone of affectionate reproach. But Spin did not move, staring at the gun with those wide eyes, quiver-ing with fear. So I took him in my arms—he trembled like a frightened child, squeezing his eyes shut so as not to see the gun which Mameli had slung over his shoulder—and we slowly climbed the stairs and emerged into the lobby.

Waiting for us were the apostolic nuncio in Belgrade, Monsignor Felici, and the minister of the United States to Yugoslavia, Mr. Bliss Lane. They had heard about my arrival, and, knowing that I was scheduled to leave for Budapest later that day, they had come to the legation to ask me to take some parcels to Budapest.

Bliss Lane had a big yellow envelope in his hands which he wanted delivered to the legation of the United States in Budapest, then he gave me the text of a telegram which he asked me to send from the Hungarian capital to his wife, who was staying with a friend in Florence. And Monsignor Felici wanted me to take a parcel to the apostolic nunciature in Budapest.

First of all we have to take care of Spin, who is very sick, I said. *Afterward, we can talk about your parcels.*

Oh, certainly, said Monsignor Felici, *first of all we need to think about Spin.*

Who is Spin? asked the minister of the United States, turning the big yellow envelope in his hands.

Who is Spin? Don't you know who Spin is? said Monsignor Felici.

Spin is sick, and we have to take care of him, I said.

I hope you are not going to shoot him, said Bliss Lane, nodding at the gun which Mameli held in his shaking hands.

It will only take one cartridge, I said.

But that's horrible, exclaimed Bliss Lane, indignantly.

Meanwhile I had gone out into the garden and laid Spin down on the gravel of the pathway, holding on to his leash. At first, he tried to escape, and struggled to free himself from the leash, whimpering softly with his child's voice. But when he saw Mameli open the gun, and slip a cartridge into the barrel, Spin curled up on the ground, trembling, and closed his eyes. Monsignor Felici turned his back, moved a few paces away with his head bowed.

Are you ready? I said to Mameli.

Everyone stood clear—Guidotto, Prince Ruffo, Count Fabrizio Franco, Bavai, Costa, Corrado Sofia—all staring silently at the gun which Mameli clenched in his trembling hands.

What you are doing is terrible, said Bliss Lane in a strained voice. *A terrible thing.*

Mameli slowly lifted his gun. Everyone held their breath. Spin, flat on the ground, was crying softly.

Fire! I ordered Mameli.

He put the gun to his shoulder, took aim, fired.

The gunshot echoed short and clear around the walls of the garden. A flock of sparrows took off with a high trill of fear.

Mameli had aimed at the trunk of a tree. A few leaves fell from its branches, floating gently in the grey air.

Spin pricked up his ears, opened his eyes and looked around: a familiar voice had sweetly struck his ear—the friendly voice of the gun.

When Mameli had slipped the cartridge into the barrel, Spin had felt his blood run cold, waiting for that crack of thunder to burst from the mouth of the gun—that dreadful roar which had overturned nature, collapsed the world, disgraced the Earth with ruins and mourning. He had closed his eyes, trembling, in agonized anticipation. But instead the gun spoke with its old familiar voice, finally cured of that monstrous madness. Everything must therefore have returned to the previous order, to the old harmonies. Nature was no longer deposed by the enormous, terrible, delirious voice of the gun gone mad, but had now begun once more to smile serenely.

Spin got up, wagged his tail, looked around—astonished and a bit disbelieving—then shook himself and ran around and around the garden, jumping with loud joyful yelps, until he came over and placed his two paws on Mameli's chest, barking happily at the gun.

Mameli was a little pale.

Let's go, Spin, he said. And followed by his dog, he walked off to hang up his gun on the corridor wall.

Sleepwalking

(1959)

In the late 1940s, when his mother was dying, Malaparte
returned home to a part of Italy he had visited only infrequently
since he ran away in 1914 (aged sixteen) to fight with the
Légion Garibaldienne in France.

So this is my native country,
the land where I was born a foreigner,
the home where I came to know the loneliness
of the outsider, the solitude
of hope, the struggles
of becoming a man.

And it was here I died,
that first time, and descended
to the streets of that other country,
the country of the dead,
and lifting my eyes I saw rivers
flowing through the sky, and the roots of trees
hanging like brown forests
in the vaulted ground above my head.

I saw animals before they were animals:
white shadows, already warm, and running,
eager to become horses, dogs,
sheep, and cattle.
And I saw the shadows of people
newly dead:
white shadows, already cold,
and lying still.

The landscape above was so delicate
that even a casual glance
could pry open the tender canvas
of its hills, trees, and walls,
revealing that mysterious country beneath,
crowded with the ghosts of trees,
the white ghosts of trees, houses, animals, and stones,
of horses, dogs, and sheep.
Crowded, too, with the ghosts of men and women,
white ghosts from the canvases of Filippino Lippi,
Sandro Botticelli, and Leonardo.

After many years, I had returned
to face that world forbidden to me for so long,
the secret country of my childhood,
traversed so many times with Edo,
months after he had died, poor Edo,
pale and delicate,
with his sad and affectionate voice.

To confront that time of my childhood
when I would slip naked from my bed
and sleepwalk through the night
between Santa Lucia and Le Sacca,
impelled by some deep fever.

My brother Sandro had shown me the way.
I would watch him slide from beneath the covers
and venture out into the yard, asleep,
open the gate at the bottom of the garden
and wander through the priest's orchard
and the Mannocci farm, still asleep,
toward Le Sacca.
But he would always return before dawn,
slipping silently back into bed,
perspiring, oblivious.

One night he reached for my hand
and we left the house together
to roam through the countryside, asleep
in the warm nights of spring,
each night for many nights.

Then he fell sick.
And when he was cured,
he was also cured of his habit.
But I continued, alone,
and he would now follow at a distance
to make sure that nothing befell me,
afraid that I might wake suddenly
in the middle of a field.

Every morning I would find myself back in bed,
exhausted, fevered, cold, and wet,
with only a vague memory of the night,
as of a marvelous voyage,
indistinct and remote.

The families in the neighboring farms
were told about me,

warned not to be taken by surprise.
for they went out often to hunt for the dead,
whom they found wandering through the fields at night,
sometimes approaching the houses,
crouching down near the door
making strange, sweet, piping lamentations.

Certainly I must have wandered
with those pallid nocturnal larvae,
with Edo, and with a nephew of the Benelli family,
a tobacconist from Santa Lucia
who killed himself with a pistol to the heart
on his sixteenth birthday.

And it is certain that I learned from them
all the marvelous things that fill my books,
secrets which are known only to the dead.
Certainly I learned from them
my way of looking at a landscape,
a tree, a house, an animal, a stone.
And certainly I learned from them
those hidden tongues of nature:
the languages of inanimate things
as well as the animate;
the speech of stones, trees, reeds, water:
speech more poetic than ours,
more serene, pure, and harmonious.

I would wander also with the dogs
who had been my companions while they were alive.
And sometimes with a ghost from Filettole,
a tailor who had been stabbed to death
behind del Gatti's bakery.
He was small and thin,

pale, with deep black eyes,
and he walked a little stooped,
still holding the knife wounds in his stomach.

We would amble up toward Le Sacca,
passing by the villa Fossombroni,
and from there we would walk along the Bardena
as it flowed through the pine forest of Monteferrato,
down toward Figline and Galceti.

Edo would hold my hand,
and every so often he would turn to look at me,
smiling, and talk in his thin, strained voice
about the sadnesses of his life
up there, in the world, where the word *life*
held no meaning for him,
unless it was one of memory and remorse.
It was from Edo that I learned to face certain facts
about life and death,
and not to fear the dead:
I, who had always had such a profound,
inexplicable fear of death.

But those nightly journeys also left me with a bitter residue
of suspicion, as well as an affectionate pity
for those who lived aboveground,
for their sadnesses, for their cruelty,
for their obstinacy in making others suffer,
as well as themselves.
More than anything I was left with a hatred of all power,
all glory, all vanity.

It finally reached the point that my parents
locked me in my room

and laced me to the bed at night,
forbidding me to follow the beckoning voices
of Edo, and the dogs, and Benelli,
and the neighing of the blind horse from Agenore's farm,
suffocated by sulfuric acid.

But when I became restless in my sleep
my brother Sandro would understand,
and shake me gently,
without waking me,
untie the laces,
open the door to our room,
and follow me outside at a distance
through the moonlit countryside.

Then, one night, my fever ended.
Ended as suddenly as it began:
a hunter, some cousin of Agenore's,
surprised me walking through the trees
as he was returning home at dawn.
He was afraid,
and because the living are afraid of the dead,
he shot at me.

I fell like a stone, hit in the shoulder,
and for two days hovered like Orpheus
at the threshold of that forbidden kingdom.
On the third day,
I stepped back into the world of the living,
marked by a scar which I carry still.

Everything I have since become
I owe to those friends from the other side:
to Edo, and Benelli,

to my dead dog, and the tailor from Filettole,
and to the blind horse from Agenore's farm.

And now that I see before me, once again,
those waves of olive trees
flashing silver in the surging wind,
and catch the distant glistening of the Arno,
the Bisenzio, and the Ombrone,
the rivers of my youth,
I am filled with love,
with an ancient love for those dear, pale, dead ones
who wander beneath my feet
and rest entwined among the roots of trees,
incorrupt,
incorruptible.

Xian of Eight Rivers

(1958)

China is made of earth, of sun-dried mud.

In this part of China everything is made from the earth:
the houses, the walls around cities and villages,
the tombs scattered over the countryside.
Even the people.

There are hills below that appear to be piles of mud
set out to dry in the sun, naked,
without a single tree or bush.
They crowd around the landscape
like the coils of bulging intestines
tossed on the ground outside butchers' shops,
slowly unraveling.

Sometimes we fly so low that we almost touch them.

And then I notice that the wind has brushed
some kind of pattern into the earth: a mysterious alphabet
written in the mud,
struggling to communicate something precise.
But there is not a single animal
or human being in the yellow desert below.

Not a single village.

Suddenly we are landing: Xian,
the geographic center of China,
where Chinese civilization was born,
in the cradle of the Yellow River.

In front of the terminal,
three children are playing with a lump of earth:
they are bundled up in jackets
and brightly printed cotton trousers.
I join them in their game
until a young woman comes out of the terminal
to call me in for dinner.
One of the children grabs me by my overcoat,
to keep me from leaving.
So do the other two, clinging to me,
asking me not to go.

The young woman comes out again,
and yells at them to stop.

They let go, disappointed.
One of them calls to me as I turn away:
Come back soon!

We eat quickly and then prepare to take off for Lanchow.
My three new friends wave goodbye to me. The littlest one
gives me a present: a pebble,
a precious gift.
In this part of China there are no stones.
You have to go to Karelia to find stone,
very far north; or to the Caucasus;
or to southern Siberia, along the slopes of the Pamir,
slanting toward the steppes of Central Asia.

I put the pebble in my pocket,
to take back home, to show what a precious gift
I was given by a little Chinese girl: a pebble
from the cradle of Chinese civilization.

A civilization made of earth,
a civilization without bones,
without a skeleton for support.
A civilization of assembled customs,
which suddenly unravel,
dissolving into thousands of separate gestures,
thousands of calligraphic icons,
thousands of smells, colors, flavors,
thousands of different shades. And then just as suddenly
they solidify again into tradition, memory, habit.

It is this absence of stone, of solid, durable material,
which makes China such an exquisite thing.
Everything is reflected:
an unimaginable number of movements,
of patterns, thoughts, images,
of which we see the copies in immense numbers,
but never the originals.

The originals were destroyed long ago.

Here are the four elements out of which China is made:
Earth, Wood, Porcelain, Silk.
The most durable of these is Silk.

I should add a fifth element: Poetry,
which is the most durable of all.

Afterword by
Lawrence Weschler

It seems to me that Walter Murch, our host and interpreter-guide across this remarkable volume, does a perfectly splendid job of introducing us to his correspondent, Curzio Malaparte, easily one of the most confoundingly astonishing writers of the twentieth century, but some readers might benefit from an introduction to Murch himself—especially those Italianists or poetry-in-translation aficionados among us who might otherwise never have heard of him, or at any rate may not have immediately realized how thoroughly familiar they already are with his own masterly production. Hence my own brief intervention in the paragraphs that follow.

But where to start? For Walter Murch, for all his self-characterization as "a rather phlegmatic phellow," is one of the most variously polymath characters around.

To begin with, there's his day job. Born in 1943, son of the Canadian painter Walter Tandy Murch, he went on to study filmmaking at the USC Graduate School in the mid-sixties among the likes of George Lucas, John Milius, and (over at UCLA) Francis Ford Coppola, on whose 1969 film, *The Rain People,* Murch started his own career editing and mixing sound. He went on to work in similar fashion on Lucas's first commercial film, *THX 1138* (based on a story Murch himself had cowritten while back at USC), and then on Lucas's breakthrough *American Graffiti,* following that up with managing (or, as he was coming to characterize his activity, "designing") sound on Coppola's first *Godfather* film.

Perhaps not surprisingly, Murch worked exceptionally closely with Coppola on their next film, *The Conversation,* for which he edited both sound and picture (a film that lost out that year to Coppola's other entry, *The Godfather Part II,* for which Murch had also edited the sound). Though already frequently nominated, Murch garnered his own first Academy Award for the remarkable sound design of *Apocalypse Now* (the extraordinary 5.1 sound innovations that Murch and Coppola pioneered in that film would quickly become the industry standard).

Over the years, Murch has worked with a host of other premier directors as well, including Fred Zinnemann (*Julia*), Philip Kaufman (*The Unbearable Lightness of Being*), Anthony Minghella (*The Talented Mr. Ripley, Cold Mountain,* and *The English Patient,* for the last of which he was awarded an unprecedented two Academy Awards, for both picture and sound editing), and Sam Mendes (*Jarhead*). He is revered among film people, and his thin, almost immaculate volume on that editing, *In the Blink of an Eye,* is a veritable bible at film schools (though its Zen-like aperçus and wider worldview thoroughly reward study by readers with no interest in film or editing). He is in constant demand at film festivals and symposia, and at one such gathering in Belgium recently, after he had been holding forth for over six hours on the intricacies of his métier, his host intervened to halt the proceedings, explaining to the audience that surely their speaker deserved a little rest, at which point the audience booed the host!

But as I say, that's only half the Murch package. Just as impressive, perhaps even more so, is how far his ever-churning mind tends to wander when he is not editing—or perhaps it's better to say, from the original occasion of his editing. As, for example, in his "law of two-and-a-half"—too complicated to enter into in detail here, though it is well worth the mind detour (see http://transom.org/?page_id=7006)— how the human brain can track only two and a half instances at a time (say, two conversations and a door knock, or the footfalls of two heavy robots lumbering across a screen in opposite directions). Any more than that (three conversations, or three robots), and it all becomes a blur (handy, for example, when, as in *THX 1138*, once you have three or more robots rumbling about, you no longer have to match footfall sounds precisely, one to the next—you can just lay in a pandemonium of foot clatter, and no one will be able to tell the difference; crucial when one is layering in six separate sound streams in the Valkyrie helicopter-attack scene in *Apocalypse Now* and one keeps having to vary the constantly shifting cacophony of sound, raising some streams, subduing others, or else everything keeps threatening to devolve into unintelligible chaos). How all of that must relate to those primitive tribes who anthropologists report have words for "one" and "two," but after that it's just "many" (or, for example, the Chinese ideogram for "forest," which turns out to be three trees).

Murch is the sort of fellow who in casual conversation is likely to introduce you to such essential (how could you have lived without knowing them before?) notions as *apophenia* (the rampant tendency of human beings to discern patterns where there are no patterns) or *apoptosis* (the regulatory process in a normally functioning body wherein a precancerous cell is encouraged to simply commit suicide), the latter in the context of an argument for replacing, in discussions of the current financial crisis, the benign-seeming, regulation–not–requiring word "bubble" with a more accurate and intervention-mandating characterization: "tumor" (see http://articles.latimes.com/2010/may/23/opinion/la-oe-weschler-bubble-20100523). Or else to regale you with the fact that for a few days in June 1600, two twenty-eight-year-olds (born within a few months of each other) found themselves jostling along together, sharing a coach on the post road between Prague and Vienna: Johannes Kepler, soon to achieve fame as the greatest astronomer of his time, and Friedrich Rosenkrantz, a ne'er-do-well cipher who would even sooner achieve fame, of a sort, as the basis for one-half of that pair of bit players in Shakespeare's *Hamlet* (the pair reprised, yes, a few centuries later as the central protagonists in Tom Stoppard's *Rosencrantz and Guildenstern Are Dead*). This as a side path off of one of Murch's greatest recent passions, an elaborate attempt to resurrect a long-abandoned bit of astronomical speculation, first advanced by Johann Titius in 1766 and refined by Johann Bode a few years later, which by means of a fairly unwieldy formula purported to predict the successive occurrence of planet orbits around a central sun—a formula that enjoyed a certain vogue for several decades (correctly anticipating the discoveries, in their correct positions, of the asteroid Ceres and the planet Uranus), before falling into ignominious disrepute when Neptune failed utterly to fit the pattern and the great mathematician Gauss seemed to have eviscerated its central tenets.

Not so fast, Murch has lately been saying: rejiggering and thereby clarifying the formula (at which point it suddenly coincides uncannily with that of the Pythagorean octave!) and extending the evidence pool to include the moons circling planets, and the recent spate of exoplanets orbiting far distant stars, proves the formula in fact accurate a remarkable 70 percent of the time, and what's up with *that?* (For more on which, see, for example, http://bldgblog.blogspot.com/2007/04/heliocentric-pantheon-interview-with.html.)

When not dabbling in gravitational astroacoustics in such a fashion, Murch is likely to take to wondering, for example, on a per-volume basis, which emits more energy, the human brain or the sun? And then to take out a pad and pencil to work out the solution. (Turns out that on such a basis, the human brain emits fifty-six thousand times more energy than the sun. And that's not just *his* brain; that's any old average human brain: yours, mine too.)

And then, in his spare time, as a change of pace and to pass the time of day, he translates Malaparte. Though, then again, not that great a change of pace. As Murch himself describes in his introduction, his method of turning Malaparte's prose into poetry draws profoundly on his film- and sound-editing practice. And the tone he achieves (granted, as a non–Italian reader I can testify in this regard only to a certain extent, but I speak out of a vivid appreciation for the rest of Malaparte's translated oeuvre), the sound, the cadences, and the rhythms, all seem to me pitch-perfect. (Murch told me how recently he'd at last gotten to see a rare Italian edition of Malaparte's own poems, and how gratified he'd been to find that the way they lay on the page, the lengths of the line, the distribution of the spaces, and so forth, all tracked with his own intuitive approximations. I was not the least bit surprised.)

Somewhere in *The Conversations*, Michael Ondaatje's marvelously wide-ranging compendium of interactions with Murch from around the time Murch was helping adapt Ondaatje's *The English Patient* into film, Murch avers how, as with such other temporally driven vocations as brain surgery, cooking, and conducting, he prefers to edit standing up (naturally, he has an elaborate theory about this as well). When thinking or writing, he goes on to note, he prefers to do so lying down. I recently asked him about translating, and that, he told me, he does sitting up. And indeed, it seems to me, these translations arise at the very midpoint of Murch's vast capacities, drawing equally on precision and imagination (the true master, as Nabokov once noted, having to evince "both the passion of a scientist and the precision of a poet").

And thus we get this volume, uncanny transmutations from the voice of one of the twentieth century's most exquisitely unreliable of narrators, which ring more than just pitch-perfect, they ring true.

Printed in the United States
by Baker & Taylor Publisher Services